Under the Blazing Stars

BECCA SEYMOUR

RAINBOW TREE PUBLISHING

UNDER THE BLAZING STARS

LOVE ABROAD COLLECTION

BECCA SEYMOUR

RAINBOW TREE PUBLISHING

ALSO BY BECCA SEYMOUR

Zone Defense

No Take Backs | No More Secrets | No Wrong
Moves

Fast Break

Rules, Schmules! | Facts, Smacts! | Regular
Smegular

True-Blue

Let Me Show You | I've Got You | Becoming Us |
Thinking It Over | Always For You | It's Not You |
Our First & Last | Next For Us

Outback Boys

Stumble | Bounce | Wobble

Fangs & Felons

Thicker Than Water | Weaker Than Instinct

Stand-Alone Contemporary

Not Used To Cute | High Alert | Realigned |
Amalgamated | Under the Blazing Stars

CHAPTER 1

ALEC

Something's wrong with me. Picking up one-and-done hook-ups has always been my thing. Yet here in Bali, not even halfway through my much-needed vacation, the only person who keeps my attention is Patrick.

Sure, his flirting game is on point. It always is. But there's something different, and the only "something" that's changed in this scenario is me. My reaction. My desire to spend time with him.

What the hell am I meant to do with that?!

"Ten o'clock for jet skiing tomorrow, right?"

I blink rapidly, only just realising I totally zoned out and was probably staring at Patrick like a confused fool. "Yeah. We'll grab a taxi at nine thirty. Should give us plenty of time."

He bobs his head and angles his beer, taking a hefty gulp. A smile tilts his lips high. "You sure you don't mind me being pillion, Alec?"

My heart flips over and I swallow hard. The fuck is happening?

For years Patrick has made it his mission to flirt with me. He's made no secret that he loves to see me blush. It's always been with good humour, though. Harmless teasing. Never has he actually come on to me or even asked for a kiss.

But why would he, since I've never given him any indication that he has my attention. Hell, that any guy has had my attention, for that matter.

"No, it's fine." I clear my throat, trying to push my imagination aside at what it's going to be like to have Patrick pushed up against me, holding me tight. Escaping the visuals by winding him up seems like a great idea, so I relax my shoulders, saying, "I'll see how many flips we can manage." I wink and start to chuckle when he widens his eyes before he narrows them, picking up that I'm teasing him right back.

The narrowed-eyed stare disappears, and he quirks a brow at me. "All the more reason for me to be pinned so tight to your arse that you'll miss me when I have to let go."

And there it goes again. A heart flip followed by

so many wings in my gut, I think I might take off. I should tease back. He expects it, as it's how I've always reacted. Sure, I blush like I've spent too much time in the Aussie sun around him, but that doesn't mean I don't enjoy dishing it back.

With my brain ensnared by his words and visuals, I don't have it in me. For the life of me, I don't understand what's changed. Why now do I like the idea of Patrick clinging to me? Why, two days ago when he rubbed sunscreen into my skin, did it feel like I was touched by a live wire? And yeah, I got hard. like full-on erection that took me twenty minutes to breathe away.

Not that it's really the first, if I'm truly honest with myself. Years of being flirted with hasn't gone unnoticed, and my mind has roamed a time or two. Maybe it's because on day one, a bartender made his interest in Patrick super clear, and the thought of seeing him getting it on slammed distress into me so hard, my knees nearly buckled. Yeah, that's something I don't want to see.

"Grub's up."

I startle at my brother's voice, grateful he's cut through my brain fart and inability to function. "Excellent. I'll grab the salad."

"See where Charlie's at as well," he says.

Nodding, I jump up and head indoors. What I need is space and the chance to collect myself.

It's not that I'm freaked about the getting hard for Patrick. Well, not totally. It's more that I don't understand why, at thirty-four, my cock's responding to him. We've known each other for years. As one of my brother's old housemates from uni, Patrick is a familiar face and a good guy. I also know him well enough to enjoy spending time with him, and even though we don't see each other often, I consider him a friend.

Maybe it's just that I have thoughts of unrequited affection on my brain.

Ross, my mate from work, is crushing pretty hard on his own brother's best friend. The guy recently showed back up in town, unearthing a shitload of feelings in Ross. Now here I am, aware my own brother's best mate has a thing for me—well, if the years of him flirting with me is to be trusted—which has started to make me think. That has to be it.

Am I a little lonely and think a relationship would be kind of nice? Maybe a bit.

Am I realising that with Patrick's flirting comes a healthy slice of sweetness and thoughtfulness? Probably a lot.

Yesterday, he made me the perfect coffee and

even managed to scrounge up some mangosteen. I've only eaten the delicious fruit in Bali before, and I may have gone on about them. And Patrick, being his awesome self, located some at the market and prepared them for a snack just for me.

There are also the small touches that have started to get my fire burning a bit brighter. Truth is, I'm liking the contact and enjoying his interest. It feels like more than simply craving attention, though.

Last night's dream of me making out with him kind of confirmed it. Waking up with a raging hard-on this morning, I was oh so tempted to seek him out. Constantly imagining what kissing him would be like is just another nail in the coffin of my interest being absolutely piqued.

Hell knows what I'm going to do about this intense attraction, though. Do I simply offer to suck him off? And don't even get me started that the idea of giving Patrick head only makes me nervous in the "will I even be any good at it?" way, rather than the "dude, aren't you straight?" quandary. Maybe I should wear supertight shorts and wiggle my arse or some shit?

I am so not good with this and am way out of my depth.

Trevor hollers my name, so I quickly pull the

prepared salad out of the fridge, call for Charlie, another of my brother's friends, and head outside.

We stayed in tonight. I was enjoying taking some time off from the bars and clubs. I'm beginning to feel every one of my years. When we're out and I see eighteen-year-olds getting it on, awkwardness slams into me. I could have taught so many of the Aussies partying in Bali this summer.

I shudder at the thought.

Placing the salad on the table, I sit opposite Patrick as Trevor sets down the chicken he's barbequed. "Good job, bro. Not burned to cinders."

Trevor flips me off—his usual sign of sibling affection. "You can cook next, arsehole."

"What? I said good job."

Patrick chuckles. "I wonder what your schoolkids would think about you if they saw you interacting with Trev."

"Ha. They'd realise that there's no hope for mankind and true maturity is impossible if they have brothers." It's true. "Alec the big brother," who still on occasion likes to pin his brother down until he taps out, is so far removed from "teacher Alec." Sure, I have fun with the kids. Most of the time. Being a PE teacher helps with my relaxed vibe. I'm hoping the new role I'm taking on next month when I get back to work doesn't change that too much.

"I reckon having a sister is a hell of a lot worse." Swiping a chicken breast, Patrick places it on his plate. I pass him the salad. "Thanks."

"You think a sister is worse than having this clown for a brother?"

Once again, Trevor flips me off. I fake catch it and put it in my pocket.

"Hell yes." Patrick accepts the mustard I've passed him with a smile and a little eye contact that makes my pulse race. Not that he asked for the mustard, but I know he likes it with his chicken. The combination is weird, but still, I made sure it was on the table. "Try sleepovers with eight fourteen-year-old girls." He shudders, and I screw up my nose.

"Okay, knowing what year nine girls can be like, especially at school camp, I totally would not have wanted to experience that."

"Right. Growing up with my sister and her gaggle of friends made me realise super early on that I could never work with kids."

I snort, thinking about Patrick's profession. He's a geologist, which sounds all levels of exciting and hot. But since my brother is too, and they both use their degrees for jobs in the mines, I know for a fact it's not all that exciting.

"Rocks or kids," I tease. "I can see how the balance would have weighed in favour of rocks."

Patrick smirks as he chews.

"That means I must have been saintly, since you experienced all this perfection"—Trevor indicates himself—"and decided teaching was your dream job." He tips his bottle of beer up to me. "You're welcome."

I scoff loudly. "As if. You were such a pain in the arse that I figured if I could survive you and keep you in line, a class of thirty kids would be a piece of piss."

Laughing, Patrick knocks his beer bottle to mine. "He didn't lose that quality all the way through uni."

"Bloody hell. Remind me again why I thought it was a good idea for you two to be here together?" There's zero heat in Trevor's attempt to sulk.

"What, us?" Patrick presses his palm to his chest. There's nothing innocent about his tone. "We make the perfect pair. Honestly, I don't know how we've both survived not seeing each other for two years."

Charlie steps out onto the wooden patio, his phone to his ear. He rolls his eyes as he listens to whoever is on the other end of the call.

"Two years?" Turning my attention back to

Patrick, I scrunch my brow, trying to recall the last time we saw each other.

"Yep. Trev's thirtieth."

"Damn." I nod. "I didn't realise it was that long. That was a good weekend."

Patrick's smile doesn't reach his eyes. I don't like the look on him at all.

Thinking back to Trevor's birthday, I'm sure it was a great party. We visited the Gold Coast, drank beer, went on a boat trip, and partied at a club. Pretty sure I hooked up that night too. Not that I recollect who or the finer details.

Patrick had been in my orbit for most of the weekend. I do recall that. We teased. He flirted. We laughed. My heart stutters when a memory rushes to the surface. It's a moment that seemed insignificant. Until now.

Patrick looking… damn, looking sad. Him glancing away and barely maintaining eye contact. It was when I was dancing with someone.

While I did absolutely nothing wrong, it doesn't stop the strange unease in my stomach, especially not when Patrick might be thinking about that night and the same memory.

Tension pulls taut between us. I don't know what to do with the invisible cord. Will it snap? Flex and settle? All I know for sure is I like it when Patrick smiles. When he's genuinely happy and relaxed.

"—tomorrow?"

"What?" Dragging my attention to Charlie, I frown, missing completely what he said.

"Tomorrow's mine and Pat's last night. Thought we'd hit a club."

The words are a smack to my face. How has the time passed by so quickly? While I'm not heading home, courtesy of my awesome summer holidays, the reminder that Patrick's leaving doesn't sit right.

"Sounds good." Trevor's up for it, apparently. Not that he's rushing off anytime soon. He managed to score a month off work and will still be here over Christmas and the New Year when our folks will fly in.

Unable to resist, my gaze finds Patrick. My eyes widen when I realise he's staring at me. And shit, I recognise that look… his expression. It's one I'm familiar with from him. What's new is how I'm sure I'm peering at him in exactly the same way.

It's one of longing.

Unsaid words. Regrets.

Something's wrong with me. I swallow hard, calling bullshit.

Nothing is wrong with me. Nope. The only thing

possibly wrong about any of this is letting Patrick walk away for another two years without me finding a way to finally kiss the longing off his handsome face.

And isn't that a "holy fucking shit" moment? I want to kiss Patrick Boundary.

CHAPTER 2

PATRICK

Glutton for punishment. Those words should be added to my obituary. Not that I plan to keel over anytime soon. Though if it's really possible to die from blue balls because of crushing on the man I can never have, then that'd be totally fitting. But back to me being a glutton for punishment.

The reason for the title has to do with my foolish pursuit of straight guys. Correction. *One* straight man.

Alec Rose.

For twelve long years, my best mate's brother has starred in practically every fantasy I've had.

Massage… oops… his cock slips inside my arse. Alec the masseur.

Swimming adventure mishap with a huge wave. Yep. Alec gives me mouth-to-mouth.

Shower with soap that refuses to stay in my hands. I'd best bend over. Oh no… is that Alec who takes me from behind?

Now, it's become something of a game. Not my sexual fantasies, but me flirting outrageously, just to see the big guy blush. The thing is, he takes it all in his stride. Even attempts sweet, flirty moments back at times, but it's crystal clear he's into women.

Every time I've seen him hook up, I wish I could erase the moments from my memory. Not that I'm holding out for my straight crush to miraculously be into cock. Specifically, my cock.

I get around and hook up plenty, but Alec Rose… I expel a frustrated sigh as I watch the dark-haired woman stroke his arm. Yeah, there's something about this hunk of man that just does it for me. My breath catches when he flicks his gaze to me. His stare is unwavering, intense, and a crackle of energy zips between us.

He jolts a little, and I lose his eyes when he peers down, clearly listening to the woman speak. This is getting ridiculous. A few shared glances and imagined chemistry are going to unravel me until I'm nothing but an empty shell if this keeps up.

"You want to get out of here?"

Trev's question has me jerking my head in his

direction. Fortunately, he doesn't look pissed off that I've been eye fucking his big brother rather than listening to whatever he has to say.

"No, I'm good." I smile, sort of meaning it.

It's the last night of my vacation in Bali. I flew out with Charlie, another friend from my uni days who Trev and I are still tight with. Charlie's nowhere to be seen, having met up with a woman he's been hooking up with for the past week. It leaves me, Trev, and Alec in a club—with Alec about to get lucky, me pining from afar, and Trev…

I pull my head out of my arse to ask, "Are you okay?" He's been a little quiet tonight.

"Yeah. Just a bit too much sun today."

Poor Trev doesn't go a gorgeous bronze like his brother. He takes after his English mum that way, where Alec's much more like his dad—not only in his solid build and height, but with his ability to tan.

"We can get going if you need an early night?" Not that it's so early. It's close to eleven, which is late for me these days but early for Bali's club-goers. Twelve-hour shifts on a two-on-two-off roster are a killer if I'm not fast asleep before ten at night. I swear, sometimes I feel fifty rather than thirty-two.

"It's your last night. You don't want to head back early."

A quick glance at Alec still having his arm stroked, and the thought of heading back to the villa doesn't seem like a drag. "Honestly, I don't mind."

Trev studies me. "How about one more drink, then we go back?"

I nod. "Sure, we can do that."

We make our way to the busy bar in La Favela after draining our bottles. As we wait in the noticeably young crowd, heat hits my back. I'm a large enough guy to not get intimidated easily; it helps that the atmosphere is pretty relaxed and focussed on having fun in the Brazilian-themed club. I freeze, assessing, before warm breath brushes against my neck, along with a voice that has goosebumps breaking out.

"You getting a drink?"

I smile, shoulders relaxing despite the awareness rippling across my skin. "You know it, handsome. Watching you all night is thirsty work." I angle to peer at Alec, enjoying how close and comfortable he is, even standing in kissing distance to me.

"We're just getting this one and going to head back to the villa," Trev adds from my side.

A crease forms between Alec's eyebrows, and he looks at me. "But it's your last night, Patrick."

Fuck, he's so gorgeous. He can't pout for shit, but that makes him even more adorable.

"You seem to be doing just fine by yourself," I tease, flicking my gaze to the brunette all but hanging off his brawny arm. I've seen up close and personal the strength in his guns, having played more than a few friendly games of footie with him. Bloody hell, Alec looks mighty fine in a pair of footie shorts.

Rather than smiling, which I'd hoped to draw from him, he furrows his brows deeper. "Shit, sorry. I've been rude." Something flickers in his gaze, and it seems like there's more he wants to say. "I didn't think. It's your last night. I came here with you guys," he ends with, but I don't think those were the words he was mulling over.

Guilt bubbles in my gut. While he's sweet as hell, he's done nothing wrong. Before I can respond, Trev says, "The sun's kicked my arse today, but if you guys want to keep hanging out, that's cool. I'll leave now and get some shuteye."

I shouldn't like the sound of that so much, but fuck if I don't want to spend some extra time swooning over Alec. Sure, Trev's one of my best mates, but we talk all the time and make sure we see each other a few times a year. It's been almost two years since I've actually seen Alec in the flesh.

He has such awesome positive energy that I don't want to miss out on any of it.

"You sure that's okay?" I ask, studying Trev.

He nods, and the relief on his features is obvious. "Go for it. I'll be up in the morning to take you to the airport for your flight back to Brisbane." After a quick back slap to both of us, Trev's out of here. Apparently more tired and eager for bed than I realised.

It leaves me now facing Alec. Our bodies are close in the noisy crowd. Thumping music surrounds us, and the line to the bar isn't showing any signs of movement. He's staring at me, a happy smile on lips I've fantasised kissing.

"So, drink?" I ask, trying to keep the slight tremble out of my voice. Our proximity is pretty damn heady.

"I've got a better idea."

I jolt at the brunette's voice, having forgotten her existence. From the slight jerk of Alec's head, I grin, pretty sure he'd forgotten too.

Not being an arsehole, I smile down at the woman. "What's this better idea of yours?"

Her smile is wide and full of mischief. I recognise it as similar to the one I've worn a time or two in the past.

"The music sucks at the moment, and the vodka's not the best. I've got the good stuff in my suite. Why don't we carry on partying there?" Innuendo laces her words.

Colour me intrigued. I quirk a brow before glancing at Alec, wondering how he's going to react to her idea.

The epitome of cool and easy-going, Alec shrugs and bobs his head. "Yeah, sounds good." There's a slight waver in his voice that takes me by surprise, though. "Let's do that."

And holy shit, we're off. My heart hammers in my chest, and I wonder, hope, fucking pray this is an opening to something more—because of course my lusty brain goes there. Does it matter that in the twelve years of knowing the guy, nothing's happened? Apparently not.

Women don't do a thing for me. That doesn't mean I didn't give it a go and have sex with a girl when I was seventeen. It took a while to get going and was unsurprisingly awful. It reaffirmed some-thing I'd freaked out about for a couple of years. I'm absolutely gay.

But getting the chance to get my hands on Alec, if he's okay with it and is into it, with a woman as a buffer? Fuck yes, I'm in. *And* if I think I'm okay with this whole situation with confidence, I'll start to believe I can do this and come away intact.

I ignore the disapproving rumblings that I'm being desperate and playing a dangerous game. Would it be wise to walk away rather than panting after Alec as I stare at his arse strolling out of the club? Quite possibly.

But if this is the only chance I get, then I can't not take it. And, if after a couple of drinks, nothing happens, then that's okay too. Nothing's changed and I go back to pining.

We step outside into the heat. The scent of street food fills the air, and too many scooters to count zip down the narrow road, even at this hour.

"Do we need a taxi?" There are plenty of hotels around, but I'm not sure where the woman's staying.

"Yeah. I'm staying at St Regis."

My brows shoot up. Trev and Alec's family's villa isn't too far away and is a nice place, but the Regis is pretty luxurious.

It doesn't take long to hail a taxi and fly through the busy streets. We chat along the way, but nothing of consequence. I can't. Alec's pressed against my side, and I swear there's tension between us, tight enough to snap and do damage. He's weirdly quiet the whole journey.

I wonder if he's second-guessing this, wondering why I'm here.

Nerves battle with excitement. Sure, I know I'm likely setting myself up for disappointment, but Alec's a smart guy. He has to know what this could possibly lead to, right? Half an hour later, we stop outside the Regis, the door held open for us.

But I can't move. Can't take a breath.

Fear keeps me frozen. The fuck am I doing even contemplating getting out of this taxi when just the thought of watching Alec with a woman stirs the acid in my gut? It's going to wreck me, but maybe that's what I need to see to finally let him go and move on.

The woman steps out, and I part my lips to speak, not sure if I'm going to change my mind or set myself up for heartbreak. "I—"

"It's probably best if I actually head back to the villa."

I clamp my mouth shut, pulse picking up speed when Alec speaks. My head snaps to the side to face him. While he's focussed on the woman, his profile is visible. Pink highlights his cheeks, easy to spot under the lights spilling in from the hotel's drop-off zone.

"Yeah," he continues, rubbing a hand over the back of his neck—he's embarrassed. "So, uhm… thanks so much for the offer…"

Not sure I've ever seen Alec flounder or struggle for words, I lean forwards and gaze out the door. "I'm flying back tomorrow and have a really early start." Barely hearing my words over the sound of my pulse in my ears, I hope my voice is even. "Sorry if we've messed up your plans."

The woman looks nonplussed for a second, but then her features relax. "Never mind. Getting an early night and some beauty sleep isn't really a hardship." When she steps back, Alec's breathy exhale reaches my ears.

Swallowing back my hurt that Alec came to his senses and doesn't want a lick of any sexy time with me, I force a tight smile. I'm a dick and I totally set myself up. Alec's done the right thing. I know it. It doesn't stop the reality of his platonic feelings from hitting me like a punch in the gut, though.

"Good night," he says as the door closes. After giving the villa's address to the taxi driver, we're on our way. It's only a short drive, but every second that passes is torture.

I should make a joke and break the tension. I should let him know he's done the right thing, especially since I had my own doubts.

Instead, I glance out the window, unable to speak. The worry of him knowing that all the teasing I've dished out over the years covers some serious feelings for him keeps me mute. The last thing I want to do is ruin our friendship.

A bump in the road has Alec smacking his head on the ceiling. "Fuck," he grunts. It's the break in tension I desperately needed. "These roads are worse than the nightmare the floods left behind back home," he grumbles.

I pay attention to where we are in the poorly lit area. I recognise enough to know we're almost at the villa. "If you think these are bad, you should see the roads out to Roma."

"That good, huh?"

"I don't go out to see my family as often as I should, but I swear the potholes were created by cyborg moles or something."

He chuckles just as the taxi pulls up out front of the locked gate. "Says the geologist."

When the car creeps to a stop, Alec reaches into his wallet.

Wishing I didn't feel like I had to do this, I reach out and stop him with a hand to his forearm. Soft hairs press against my fingertips, and I fight to ignore my desire to stroke his warm skin.

When he angles to look at me, I forget to breathe. There's so much emotion swirling in his brown eyes that I'm not sure how to make sense of what I see. But I've got to at least try to make this right.

Taking a short breath, I say, "If you want to head back by yourself, then that's okay. I won't be offended." Devastated, sure, but I wisely keep those emotions locked down.

There are a few beats of us staring at each other before Alec speaks. "But what if I want to stay here with you?"

My throat dries. "You want to stay here with me?" He means to have an early night, maybe share a quick beer before bed, right?

"Yeah."

"You don't want to go and hook up with that woman?" I speak quietly, more than aware the taxi driver is waiting for us to pay and get out.

"No." It's all he offers before he hands the driver some cash and steps out of the car. I scramble after him, not sure what's happening here. I'm not naïve and I'm not an idiot, but with the way Alec keeps looking at me, I feel like I'm walking the edge of reality.

The muggy warmth blankets me once we're outside the locked gate. Silently, I follow Alec through into the fenced garden. The villa's positioned not far from Sawangan Beach, a little away from the pretty, albeit manic village streets.

"How about a dip in the pool?"

His question has me stumbling. So no beer or sleep? I'm down with that. Hell, the cool water will help to calm the simmer under my skin that might set me on fire any second.

"Sounds good." I follow him around to the back, bypassing the house. When we reach the pool, I say, "Let me just grab my sw—"

Bloody hell.

Alec tugs off his T-shirt, revealing sun-kissed skin wrapped around muscles.

"You coming in?"

His question makes me jolt, and I'm struggling to get my brain to catch up to my mouth. I'm so focussed on all the delicious skin before me and wondering what he's going to do without swimmers that my brain turns to mush.

"Uhm…" I clear my throat. What the hell is wrong with me? "You want me to join you without grabbing my boardies?" I wish I didn't feel the need to ask, but twelve years of crushing and flirting to now this… me seeing his cock, 'cause that's what's going to happen here, right? Hell, I can't reconcile what's changed or how we got here.

With a shrug, Alec turns to me. "We're two grown-arse men and have the same equipment." Something flickers in his gaze, and my breath catches at the way he peruses my body. When his attention snaps to mine, I swear he's breathing more heavily. Me? I'm standing stock still and can barely suck in air.

His brow furrows. "Shit, unless this is too weird?"

I shake my head, not wanting to miss out on whatever *this* is.

I tug off my tee. That Alec's gaze briefly skims over my naked chest has me carrying on. I pop open the button on my shorts, unzip, and with no ceremony whatsoever, hook them down and off.

Shame free, I'm naked and smiling. Am I nervous? My heart's flipping out a little for sure, but my cock twitches as soon as Alec's gaze falls on it.

Pink floods his cheeks, but it takes a beat for him to tear his gaze away. Unsurprisingly, my dick likes this a lot, filling even more and hardening to steel.

"I'll meet you in the pool." Alec's gaze shifts at my words and he makes eye contact. What I don't miss is the way his Adam's apple bobs.

"Okay." He nods, cheeks still flushed. But it's the look in his eyes that has me pausing and my pulse speeding up.

Fuck, is that really interest I see in his gaze? Whether it's curiosity or more, he's not running, and I'm confident the man isn't drunk so is fully in control of his decisions.

We're locked in a stare, and I don't think I can get my legs to move even if I tried harder. Admittedly, I'm more than happy to be here in this moment, energy and awareness sparking between us that I've only dreamed possible.

And then his fingers are working his button and zip, but I can't pull away from his gaze. Alec has captured me so completely that my head spins from lack of oxygen, and quite possibly from the pulse of heat spreading through my body.

Alec Rose naked is magnificent.

Inhaling air into my lungs, I'm able to function again and take in my fill. He's not running away. I trace every inch of skin with my greedy eyes, wishing I could follow the journey with my fingers and tongue.

Him standing like this, proud and thickening before me, means *something*, right? 'Cause, holy shit, I desperately hope that's what this is. While I have no idea why this is happening now, and after all this time, I'd be a fool to question or back away.

Rather than me leading the way, Alec takes the

first step in the direction of the pool. Do I ogle his toned arse? Damn straight I do.

And this right here is why I'm a glutton for punishment. I follow him. If that's not enough proof that I'm likely to get my heart wrecked and dreams crushed, then clearly I don't know shit.

CHAPTER 3

ALEC

Desire weaves through every cell in my body. I'm worked up, feeling a high I've never experienced before.

I can't even blame booze, having only had two bottles tonight.

The reality is, while the woman from earlier is pretty, when she suggested Patrick join us it startled a reaction in me that was so unexpected it took me the taxi ride over to her hotel to catch up.

A threesome is not something I've ever experienced before. Sure, I've fantasised about it, watched some porn with two holes being pounded by guys, and the truth is, I've even been given the chance more than a handful of times. Each offer I refused, not really feeling it at the time.

With Patrick, though… my cock chubs as I make eye contact with him. The coolish water does nothing to calm down my dick's eagerness. Patrick looks sexy sitting opposite me, stark naked, his attention barely leaving my body.

Yeah… there's no denying Patrick is on my mind and was all I could think about in the taxi. It was the thought of sharing Patrick with anyone that had my arse stuck to the leather of the back seat. Getting out the car had felt wrong. It was the prickle of possibility zapping between me and Patrick, though, that had me speaking up and resulted in us leaving.

A conversation I had with my friend Ross slams into me. We'd discussed this trip and my feelings about seeing Patrick.

"I just feel awkward."

"Because he's a man?"

I'd shaken my head, as that was so not it. *"It's not even that. It's that I like him… as a friend."* I'd added the clarification, despite knowing I wasn't being fully honest with myself or Ross. *"But hanging out with him makes me feel like shit because I'm worried about leading him on."* It was a good enough excuse at the time. Now, with Patrick naked and delicious before me, it's necessary to call bullshit.

My reaction to the man isn't as surprising as it should be.

We've known each other for ages, and while I like him and have enjoyed hanging out with him, it's only been the last few times seeing him I really considered how hot he is. Attractive, sure, that's something I've always acknowledged. I know a good-looking guy when I see one. But sexy and my cock reacting? I'm not quite sure what to make of it, even though since the start of this holiday that's exactly what's happened. And before then? Well, there's been chemistry for sure, and maybe a chub here and there, but not significant enough to make me consider actually doing something about it.

So fuck it.

I'm tired of overthinking. I want to go with it, follow my gut, focus on the way my skin heats when he stares at me, and do what feels right.

And from his expression and the way his dick reacted to me, there's no doubt left in my mind that his flirting over the years has been him simply teasing and getting a rise out of me. This is so much more.

The water ripples when Patrick swirls his arms around. I wish I had a beer or something. Peeling a label right now would help centre me, because I'm feeling unbelievably horny but am in unfamiliar territory. I've never had a problem hooking up or making the first move. The countless number of one-night stands is testimony to that. But here's the thing: I'm out of my depth.

There's no doubt Patrick has caught and kept my attention from day one of him joining us in Bali. Is he the person I'd like to see with their hand wrapped around my cock? Damn right. But I have no idea how to make that happen.

As for kissing? I've never kissed a man before. Tonight, and with Patrick, yeah, I'm feeling it a hell of a lot. I gaze at his mouth. His lips are fuller than mine, certainly different to any other lips I've got up close and personal with.

Mesmerised and taking my fill of Patrick, I imagine what he'll taste like, what his lips will feel like gliding against mine.

With his gaze on me, he quirks his lips. "See something you like?"

My brows shoot high and fresh heat hits me, this time in my stomach. "Well…" I can do this. "You've never tried to kiss me." I arch my brow, proud there's no shake in my voice, despite how my body's vibrating.

Fresh ripples appear around Patrick. The movement in his chest is more pronounced. "True."

It's all he gives me, which is frustrating as fuck. Jesus. I need him to take the lead on this. But for whatever reason, he's not making that easy. "Why not?"

He seems to contemplate my question. "That's the thing about being respectful and not pouncing on unattainable guys. Plus, you've never given any indication it's something you're interested in." His lips lift, and he tilts his head, his gaze roaming my shoulders.

My dick twitches at the intensity of his perusal.

"Is it something you might be interested in now?" The question is low, gruff, filled with unspoken need and promises.

My breath catches and I nod, so freaking turned on by how Patrick's looking at me like he wants to eat me up. Add in how he's taking control and coming out with the question I was desperate to hear, and I have no choice but to palm myself. Keeping my lust contained so I don't blow takes effort.

"You okay if I do that?" Patrick takes a few steps in my direction, the water at chest height lapping against his skin. His voice is low and he's clearly waiting for my okay.

Unable to speak without revealing just how

desperate I am for this to happen, I nod again, squeezing my dick hard.

He moves slowly. I want him to hurry the hell up, but fuck if his cautious movement isn't kind of sweet. Patrick's never held back from flirting with me. A few times I felt a little awkward, unsure if his flirting hid real feelings I didn't think I'd ever be able to return. Other times were awkward as my cock rose to the possibility of something actually happening one day.

What the hell would a guy like Patrick want with me when I wasn't even sure if I was bi?

Laughter bubbles in my chest, threatening to spill over as I think about it. My being uneasy and concerned has led me to this moment. With my dick close to exploding, I'm at the point of begging for Patrick to put his hands on me.

He stops before me, close enough to make my skin break out in goosebumps and for me to feel his heat.

"Hey." The word is shy and contrasts massively to the intensity in his gaze. Patrick's been in my space plenty of times, but naked, yeah, it's new and exciting.

I smile, despite my nerves. "So, this is different." Unwilling to burst this bubble we're in, my words are whisper soft.

"Okay different?"

Not wanting to answer without thought, I stare at him, take in his features, his uncertain smile, his broad shoulders, and his expanse of damp skin. "Definitely okay."

Patrick's tongue darts out, wetting his bottom lip. I follow the movement and swallow hard.

"Okay enough for me to kiss you?"

Fresh bubbles fizz to life in my stomach, loving that he asked. I've never been asked the question before. "Yeah."

He doesn't wait. Doesn't hold back.

His lips touch mine, but rather than fast and hard, the pressure is soft, almost delicate as he kisses me. Our mouths move with ease as he leads, stoking the fire in my belly until his tongue dips into my mouth, sweeping against mine. I groan, release my cock, and wrap my arms around him.

He edges closer, leaning into me eagerly. Our chests and groins touch, sparking fresh heat and urging me to devour him. But Patrick takes control, slowing down the building frenzy, keeping the connection soft, and gentle, and so deliciously perfect that I sigh into his movement, letting him take over completely.

The kiss is different, not only because he's taking

the lead, but the slight scrape of scruff against my chin. The sensation pulls a delectable shiver through me, only heightened when his large hands get in on the action.

One settles at my nape, the other on my back.

We kiss until we're breathless. We kiss until all I can taste and think about is Patrick. We kiss until the loud chirping of a gecko cuts through my lust and has us pulling away.

Wide-eyed, I stare at Patrick.

His cheeks are flushed, the pink just obvious in the low outdoor lighting. A small smile quirks his lips, and like me, he's breathing heavily.

Dragging my gaze away, but not willing to let go and break the spell or the connection, I check we're alone. Not that my brother would be pissed off if he saw us. Puzzled, maybe a little concerned, but definitely not angry. The last thing I want is for him to see me making out with his best friend, though.

I angle and search, peering at the closed bamboo doors. I wait for confusion to settle in, but all I feel is the warmth of Patrick's hands.

"I… uhm…" I'm not sure what to say.

Patrick's silent for a beat. "Do you want to stop?" I hear the hesitation, the reluctance in his tone. The sound sends a thrill through me.

By now, my brother should be fast asleep, and I can't imagine Charlie being inside.

I search Patrick's gaze. Do I want this to end? This is new and I suppose it should be perplexing, but there was nothing confusing about the kiss we just shared. Plus, my cock is so damn hard, and Patrick is the reason for that. Why on earth wouldn't I want to explore this?

And that Patrick's a man who knows what he's doing and is someone I trust, well, yeah, I don't think I could walk away even if offered a million dollars.

"I have a big bed." My words are whisper soft, not holding their usual confidence.

Patrick's lips part. I've surprised him, but rather than calling me out, he offers a pleased smile, one filled with promise, and I sure as shit hope it's a dirty one. "Let's grab our clothes." He punctuates his words with a kiss, and it's hard to pull away and get my arse moving. A squeeze of my butt cheek does the trick, especially when he trails his lips down my neck, saying, "Fuck, Alec, if only you knew all the things I want to do to your body."

My limbs tremble, pulse picking up speed. "Yeah?"

"So, so many things. I want to unravel you and put you back together again, so all you'll be thinking about is me for a long, long time." His hand drifts to my naked cock. He squeezes, tearing a deep groan from my kiss-bruised lips. "You're going to taste so delicious." He tugs on my dick, gives a couple of strokes, pulling another moan from me.

"Let's head inside."

At his words, I can barely keep myself upright as he pulls away. He's out of the pool, water trickling down his taut body. His shape's so different to my own—slimmer, more compact. The way the water drips down his skin, rolling over his muscles, getting caught in the hairs on his thighs, is mesmerizing. Moving quickly, I follow him out, finding our clothes on one of the loungers.

"I feel like I'm sneaking around and your parents are asleep inside."

Honestly, I feel the same way. The thought tugs a bark of laughter from me. It's loud in the humid night. I clamp my mouth shut, still grinning. It's awesome that he's so relaxed and that we know each other well. It's, I don't know, comforting almost.

Feeling more certain than ever that my cock's got the right idea, I grab my clothes.

A trickle of sweet energy zips between us as we dry ourselves off with one of the pool towels stacked by the door. Once we're dry, I reach out and hold his hand. It should be weird, standing here and doing this, but the touch of his skin calms me. What it doesn't do is settle my desire.

Patrick squeezes my hand, and I side-eye him as we move side by side to the door. A sexy smirk is directed my way.

"I can't believe you get to hang out in paradise for a few more weeks," he says quietly as we step into the air-conditioned living space.

I appreciate the break in tension as much as I like the normalcy of the conversation. I throw him a cocky smile. "Gotta love school holidays. Just one of the many benefits of teaching."

"Yeah? There's others?" he teases, his thumb sweeping over my knuckles as, butt-naked, we head towards my room. I seriously hope my brother doesn't decide to grab a bottle of water from the fridge.

"A few. Most of the kids are cool, you know, when they're not being arseholes." I chuckle, relieved when we get closer to my room. It's hard to not slam him against the wall and steal a kiss, but the conversation's helping to keep me composed.

"And you teach straight PE?"

I snort, and he joins in, squeezing my hand.

"You know what I mean, jackass."

"*Straight* PE… not sure I'm eligible after what just happened in that swimming pool." My smirk turns sly, my confidence rising to the surface and sitting bold as you like in my chest. It's rare I'm thrown or left floundering. Tonight has done both, but I'm keen to relax and be comfortable with this new development.

"I feel like nutting myself for saying this and potentially having you change your mind," he says, leaning in close as we finally step inside my room, "but what gives? I've always thought you were straight."

He says it how it is and what's on his mind. It's refreshing, not beating about the bush or expecting me to be a mind reader.

"Me too. Mostly." My shrug is casual, and I kinda figure I'm coming across as a clueless arsehole, which is not what I want. I clarify, "I've got to be honest, I've thought about you this way a few times, but wasn't sure what that meant. I suppose I've never really had the opportunity to explore my interest in you. I liked what we did, though."

Patrick turns to face me, moving even closer to reach behind me so he can close and lock my door.

I continue speaking, my nerves pushing me to overshare. "I hope we get to do more of it, but I have no idea what that really means, other than I suppose I'm not as straight as I thought." I glance at him. "It's up to you what you want to do about that."

Leaving it up to Patrick seems a bit like a cop out, but I can't be any clearer than I've already been. I've always liked Patrick. Hanging out with him has never been a hardship. Tonight, other than fooling around, I don't have any more answers beyond I'm interested.

"Everything." His voice pitches low, turning to gravel. "I want to do everything with you."

Jesus.

I fumble for the switch that activates one of the small lamps. Light spreads across a small section of the room, illuminating the white cotton sheets and Patrick's face.

God, he really is good-looking. Sexy, even. I still don't know why it took me so long to see it and act on it, but with him fully in my space, I'm not willing to question why now.

We move at the same time. Desire pushes me forwards, urging me on. There's no hesitation or resistance as our tongues tangle, mouths moving, giving and taking as we kiss.

He tastes incredible, even better than in the pool.

He spins me, takes a step, and eases me backwards, and I know it's in the direction of my bed.

While nerves beat at my chest, they don't scare me. The only thing I'll regret is not exploring this with Patrick.

The backs of my knees hit the mattress, again, not a position I'm used to since I usually take the lead. I smile against his lips. The movement has Patrick pulling away and grinning at me, question in his eyes.

"Your kisses are hot," I admit, my lips stretching wide.

He chuckles and tugs my clothes that I'm still clutching out of my arms. Once they're discarded, he traces his fingers over my chest, his gaze fixed on mine. "Your kisses are fucking incredible. Everything I ever imagined."

My gut fizzes at his words, my cock already at full mast from the steamy kiss. "You thought about it a lot?" I'm totally fishing. Patrick hasn't made his interest a secret over the years. In truth, I've liked his attention, but his flirting's always seemed to be just about getting a rise or a blush from me. From the way he's staring at me like he wants to gobble me up, I'm not sure how I'm going to come away from tonight unscathed.

Not going to lie. It feels good to have his eyes on me. To be at the centre of his attention.

"You good to have my weight?"

"Yeah." We're fully naked, so I know what this means. I drag in a shaky breath.

"Sex doesn't have to look the same way as it does for straight folk. It's not all about penetration." While he's teasing, his tone is gentle, reassuring. The combination settles the nerves threatening to unravel me.

"Okay, yeah," I say, exhaling before I recentre. I want this, so there's nothing to be worried or anxious about. The reminder is enough to have me easing back on the bed. Patrick quickly follows my lead, then encourages me further up the mattress with a gentle shove and a grin. He's playful and makes me smirk. And then he's pressing against me, mouth on my neck, hand on my junk, and my eyes roll back.

Sliding his hand over my chest, Patrick laps at my neck. A brush of my nipple, and I gasp. I fucking love nipple play, something that doesn't really happen with one-night stands.

Leaning up, Patrick says, "You have sensitive nipples?"

I nod. "Yeah."

"As in sensitive leave them alone or love the hell out of them?"

I dampen my bottom lip, already nodding. "The second. Definitely the second."

In answer, he grins before he goes to town on my

nipples with his hot mouth. Combined with him jerking me off, I'm a panting mess, and I haven't even touched him. Hell, I can't. I'm a bundle of need and completely at his mercy. The desire to take my fill pushes me to say, "Enough. I need your mouth back." That it means he'll shift so I can touch his dick for the first time sends a fresh wave of lust through me.

"You have no idea how fucking gorgeous you are," Patrick mumbles before he captures my mouth. This kiss is everything. He fucking owns this kiss, momentarily whiting out my mind as I get lost in the sensation of his mouth on mine.

Jesus, I'm so close to coming, even though he's stopped jacking me off. No way can I let that happen.

Needing to get some control back, even just a little, I slow the kiss and ease away. His groan makes me smile. The sound is not a happy one.

"I want to touch your dick."

My words get his attention. He puts a bit of space between us with a speed that has me chuckling.

"You ever touched a dick that wasn't your own before?" Quiet concern threads his tone, but there's longing there too. I feel it in the vibration of his limbs. In how breathless he sounds.

"No." My head shake is miniscule. "But I really want to make you come."

"Fuck." This groan is needy, desperate. He closes his eyes and holds on to his dick. Deep breaths follow.

Like this, Patrick looks hotter than I've ever seen another person, and even though I have to hold back my chuckle, that he's as eager as I am makes my dick twitch. It also gives me the confidence to move and take what I want.

I reach for him and palm his cock. His breath hitches when I wrap my fingers around silky steel that feels so right in my hand. He's heavy, firm, and feels so perfectly different.

Following my gut and what I enjoy, I sweep my fingers across the end. They glide easily when I reach his precum. My gaze snaps to his, cataloguing his reaction. His pupils are blown, eyes wide, lips parted.

I don't ask if what I'm doing is right. His expression is enough. A smug smirk curves my lips. Yeah, I'm proud as fuck to earn this reaction. My smirk is short-lived when he grips my dick and goes to town jacking me off.

"Fuck." I jerk my hips, chasing his touch, shifting in time with his movements.

I latch on to his expression. The smug smirk is on his lips this time, and I can't help but grin back, even realising my hand's stopped.

Trying hard to focus on not coming, I pour my energy into getting him off. Our hands work in tandem, and while I'm desperate to kiss Patrick, I'm more eager to see the action. I angle back just enough to peer between us. The sight of us holding each other's dicks, palms moving rapidly, is almost too much.

A groan slips free. "Jesus. So fucking hot."

"Yeah?"

I nod, unable to glance away. "Fuck yes."

My words get a reaction from him. He squeezes a little tighter, forcing a grunt past my lips, and then he's shifting, pushing me onto my back, and I lose his hand.

"No! Where—" I snap my mouth closed as Patrick takes hold of my erection and wraps his lips around me. "Holy fuck… nnghh." I fight not to look away. Fight to stop my eyes from rolling back, despite the fire already licking at the base of my spine.

Hot and wet, his mouth is unlike any I've ever experienced. Blow jobs can be the fucking best, but far too often, the mouths of the past have not gone all out. Not like this.

Spit dribbles down my balls. Heat surrounds me. I have no choice but to hold on.

My hand finds his cheek, the other the bed sheets,

but it's when Patrick groans, sending vibrations along my cock, that I know holding on is pointless.

"Fuck, fuck, fuck, gonna come."

It's barely enough warning before I shoot my load. My eyes close, hips jerk, and Patrick keeps sucking, his fingers pinching my tender balls with the perfect bite.

Empty and close to passing out, I sag against the mattress. "Holy shit," I pant. "Amazing."

I pry my eyelids open when I feel him move. Patrick's cheeks are pink as he gnaws down on his bottom lip. His hand's moving. Immediately, I glance down, not wanting to miss the action. On his knees, Patrick is jerking off. His cock's angry and so fucking lickable.

"Come in my mouth." The words are out there before I have time to question them. All I focus on is how debauched and sexy Patrick looks.

His hand stutters at my words and he groans. "Yeah?" he asks, already moving, hand back to working his dick.

"Yeah." I nod, open my mouth, and reach out for him as soon as I can get my hands on his arse.

"Fuck, Alec." His panted words are barely above a whisper. I like the sound of them, like how much he wants this.

He pauses when he's straddling my chest, his dick right before my face. The glistening head stares at me, and I swear he's huge, but damned if I can back away. I need to know what he tastes like. What it's like to feel his cum trickling down my throat.

And fuck… my cock twitches… I want to know what his skin, the weight of his cock feels like on my tongue.

I tilt my head, lifting off the pillow. With my gaze on his, I say, "Put your dick in my mouth."

His lips part as he moves. His eyes widen to the size of saucers as he leans forwards and places his cock in my mouth. I wrap my lips around him, trace my tongue along the underside of his dick, then suck.

"Oh fuck, fuck, oh fuck." Patrick shudders as spurts of warmth enter my mouth. One shot hits the back of my throat, and I swallow quickly. The second hits my tongue as Patrick eases back a little. Salty spunk—there's no questioning what this is—sits on my tongue, and I swallow again as soon as Patrick withdraws fully.

He shifts down the bed and collapses next to me. His arm lands on my chest, his face close to my neck. Heavy breaths sweep against my skin as I smile and take stock.

I swallowed cum. Made out with a man, and not

just any guy. Patrick, who I've known for years. I wait for the panic to hit me. Five, ten, fifteen breaths, and it doesn't arrive.

Patrick's breathing evens out, and I feel tension turn his muscles taut.

Frowning, I peer around, but in this position, I can't see his face. "Okay?" I ask, my tone as neutral as possible, not sure me singing in glee would be appropriate considering how tightly coiled he seems.

"Yeah." He clears his throat and angles away. Finally, our gazes connect. Uncertainty blazes in his. "You?"

I bob my head, the movement a little awkward lying down. "Yeah." A yawn escapes, not even unexpected, as coming so spectacularly always zaps my energy and makes me bone tired. "Sorry." I chuckle, rubbing a hand over my face. "Empty balls equate to nap time." Reopening my eyes after yawning, my smile dulls. "You sure you're okay?"

"Yeah, sure. It's late; no wonder you're tired."

I frown at his tone. It's like he's talking to a spooked animal. Hell, I've used a similar tone in class when one of my students have kicked off and are close to losing their shit. I just don't understand why he's using the tone with me.

"Totally worth it," I say, making it clear I

have zero regrets about what just happened. Hell, it's a night that's burned into my brain. I study Patrick, and even with his wary stare, he's totally fuckable. I am up for doing this again with him. Hell, it would be a crying shame not to explore more.

Not only do we know each other well, so there's no painful "getting to know you" to be done, but compatible isn't even close to describing how hot what we just shared was.

I smile, thinking about introducing Patrick to my friends. Ross, one of my best mates, will be gobsmacked, I swear, but he'll be supportive as hell. And if this—as in us—is something Patrick is keen to explore, Ross is the perfect friend for me to go to for advice.

Patrick moving off me catches my attention.

Realising I've been quiet for a beat too long and I probably look unhinged since I'm smiling away, it's hardly surprising. "Shit, sorry, spaced out. Just thinking about Ross and what he's going to say when I tell him about this."

Stilling his movements, Patrick's eyes widen. "You're going to tell someone what happened?"

"Well, only my friend." My eyebrows furrow. "Shit, unless you don't want me to. That's cool. Ross, my friend, he's gay. We work together and have known each other for years."

There's still distance between us, and I wish there wasn't. I liked it when Patrick was snug beside me, his breath tickling my neck.

"He's going to get a kick out of this. Hell…" I chuckle, the high of orgasming and having my mind blown by Patrick making it hard to contain myself. Energy buries my exhaustion when I look at his mouth, remembering all too clearly how it felt to be kissed by him, let alone sucked off. "I should have added tonight to my bucket list. One great big tick right here."

If there was such a thing as moon eyes, I swear that's what Patrick's seeing right now. Jesus, the more I think about tonight, our kisses, our chemistry, the more I know it's something I want to explore.

And not just this discovery about myself with any good-looking guy. Hell no. Specifically with Patrick. "Maybe we could…" My words trail off when he moves off the bed completely. "What are you doing?" The buzz thrumming through me begins to stutter and fade.

"I have an early flight tomorrow, and you're tired."

Shit. My stomach bottoms out. It really is a one-night thing. I hoped after years of Patrick flirting, I wasn't simply an itch he needed to scratch and get out of his system. I swallow hard, burying my disappointment deep in my gut.

The last thing I want is to be clingy or for this to become something weird between us.

"Right. Yeah. Sure. I uhm… I get it." Feeling exposed, I latch onto the sheet and tug it over my junk. My smile's tight. "If I don't see you when you leave, have a safe flight." The words taste bitter, which is all levels of ludicrous. Jesus, I know this routine well. Each time I've had a one-night stand, I've walked away with a smile and a whistle.

But bloody hell, this feels different. Maybe it's because we've known each other for so long. Maybe it's because he's my first experience with a man. Either way, I need to shake this off and grow a pair.

I force my shoulders to relax as Patrick studies me. Pink sits high in his cheeks, and I know it can't be sadness I see in his gaze. If it was, he wouldn't be leaving.

"I'll… yeah, I'll see you around."

He turns his back on me, revealing his perfect arse. Fuck. I look away, needing to get over myself.

I'm viscerally aware of Patrick's movements. It

only takes a few seconds before he's quietly opening the door and shutting it gently behind him.

I fall back in bed, my head landing on my pillow that smells of sweat and Patrick's aftershave. It would be sensible to get up and shower and brush my teeth. I'm just not ready to get the taste of him out of my mouth yet, nor the smell of his skin off mine.

Tugging a pillow on top of my head, I groan into the soft material.

Tonight was incredible. Life-changing. What I need to remember is that while I feel that way, Patrick absolutely doesn't. I need to find a way to make peace with that and just focus on how amazing the experience was.

In a few short weeks, I'll be back at work and taking on a new challenge with my leadership role. It means I won't have any time to pine. I just hope it doesn't take too long for me to think about tonight with a fond smile rather than an ache in my gut.

CHAPTER 4

PATRICK

THREE MONTHS LATER

Work's been manic. Between my company pissing me off by sending me to Western Australia for two months to do some investigatory work on a new quarry before heading back to the main mine in Rocky, and the general craziness of the day-to-day grind, I've barely had time to breathe, let alone get any real downtime.

It sounds crazy for sure that I grumble about having little "downtime," since I have two weeks at work, followed by two weeks off, but when you take into account the travel time between work and home, I already lose out on two days, plus there's getting on top of maintenance. I'm beginning to question why I have a house to begin with.

I seriously should have invested in an apartment. Not having five acres to deal with would make life a lot easier. Growing up on a big property outside of Roma means I'm used to space. Five acres feels tiny, and that I can see my neighbours is something I can't help but be weirded out by.

What being so busy does mean is I've buried the night with Alec far, far down, to the point where I can almost believe it was a dream. A hot, mind-blowing dream maybe, but still, not part of my reality.

It's best I think about the night that way.

If not, I'll mull over how amazing the night was. How delicious he tasted. How fucking enthusiastic he was. Carefree, even.

Only for any fantasy I may have had about a possible future together come to a screeching halt when he started talking about ticking off what we shared as some sort of bucket-list achievement.

Talk about a sucker punch.

But fuck, I'm thinking about him again, even though I need to move on.

I load my dishwasher with my breakfast crockery. It's hot out, and the rain's been relentless, which means I need to mow again. It's like a jungle out there. Two weeks away from home, and it's like my yard's been ignored for three months. The combination of sun, heat, and too many millimetres of rain is ridiculously perfect for my grass to think it's in a growing competition.

After applying sunscreen, I head out to my shed, start my ride-on mower, turn on my music, and get to work.

My arse is already sweating after twenty minutes in the autumn heat. While the sun doesn't feel as intense as where I grew up, it's more humid here outside of Brisbane. Something my body apparently still struggles with.

My phone rings, and I answer with a click of the button on my headphones, cutting off the mower's engine.

"Hello."

"G'day, Pat. How's it going?"

I smile at Trev's voice coming through my earbuds. "Good, mate. Yourself?"

"Yeah. Same old. Work and barely time to shit."

I snort. "Sounds like something I can relate to."

He chuckles before asking, "You back home?"

"Yep. Just got in yesterday."

"I'm heading out to do a spot of fishing on Saturday, if you're around."

It's been a while since we caught up, and relaxing with a rod and a beer sounds pretty sweet. It will also mean an early start, so going out the night before won't be doable. Not that I've been feeling it recently anyway. Since Bali, hooking up just hasn't had the same draw. And I hate how pathetic that sounds.

"Sure. Count me in."

"You beaut. I'll text you the details. Should just be a few of us."

I freeze, hoping to hell he doesn't say his brother. Not that I think Alec's much of a fisherman. He tends to do sports anyway on the weekends, so I should be safe.

"Yeah?" I ask tentatively.

As if reading my mind, he says, "Just Geordie and maybe Charlie."

I expel a breath, but he doesn't call me out. While Trev knows something happened between me and his brother, which he admitted to me, he hasn't asked a single question. I appreciate it more than he probably realises.

"Sounds good." And it does. I have a few different groups of friends. A couple of guys I spend time with when at work, a group of single guys I go out with in Brissie, and then Trev, who I've known since uni. He calls himself my token straight friend, but after twelve years, he's more than that, and definitely one of my best mates.

"Excellent. I need to go. Just driving to the office now. Wish me luck dealing with health and safety."

I snort. "Yeah, good luck with that. See you at the weekend."

He cuts the call, and I restart the mower. My music's already playing, having kicked in when the call ended. I sing along to the playlist Amazon Music's thrown together for me. I'm belting out the lyrics to a cheesy pop song when it's cut off by another call.

I turn off the engine and hit the button on my earbud.

"Hello."

"Pat." Just the one word makes me frown. My sister sounds breathless.

"What's wrong?"

"It's Dad. He's fallen off that damn bike of his. LifeFlight are sending him out to Toowoomba soon for surgery." Her words are rushed.

My stomach bottoms out, and I stand abruptly, unable to sit still. "Holy shit. How bad?"

"He's fine," she says quickly. "Well, needs surgery, but it's not life-threatening. He's broken his hip, and Roma hospital doesn't cater for that op. He's scheduled for an early morning operation, so they want to get him settled before they take him in."

"Jesus." I press against my chest, breathing a little easier after panic he might be at death's door. You never get over hearing that sort of news. Something my sister and I both know from experience, having received tragic news about our mum seven years back. "Okay." I take a shuddery breath, feeling a little light-headed. "Hip surgery? Shit, he's going to be out of action for a while." I grimace, thinking about how Dad will react to that news. His property doesn't run itself. I was due to be heading out soon, over Easter, to lend a hand with castrating the bull calves and getting them tagged.

"Yeah. Let's face it, he's going to be a nightmare."

Even not seeing her face, I know my sister's wincing. As one of Dad's neighbours, she sees him regularly and knows all too well he makes the worst patient. Three years ago, he ended up needing surgery on an arm fracture—because he ignored the break, kept working, and damaged it further. I had to head out for two weeks and practically sit on him to make him do as he was told.

"Right. What do you need?" Already, I'm making travel plans in my head. Figuring I'll have to head to Toowoomba, which will take just a couple or so hours, I expect I'll need to then take him home once he's been released. That's a good four hours. Stops will need to be made, I expect, due to his injury. And obviously it all depends on how long he has to stay in hospital.

Fortunately, Dad's young. Or as young as he can be for a grumpy old sod.

"I can't get there until tomorrow." I nod as my sister speaks, even though she can't see me. With three kids, she has a busy schedule. "If I make sure I'm there for his surgery tomorrow, can you see him today?"

"Of course. Once we know more from the hospital, we can then figure out a plan, okay?"

A sigh of relief travels down the line before she releases a shaky "Thanks, Pat."

"He'll be fine," I reassure her, understanding without words that she's anxious and thinking about how we lost our mum in a tragic car accident. "A hip fracture's not fun and will take a long time for recovery, but it's everyday surgery, okay?" I'm sure I'm not spouting bullshit. People get breaks all the time. It's common when you get older. With Dad not yet sixty, it's a shit of a thing, but it means he'll bounce right on back. At least, I hope that's the case.

Other than him being a grouch at times, he's fit and healthy.

Those bloody bikes need to go, though. Whether Dad likes it or not, I'm going to sell the damn things the first chance I get.

"Yeah, I know." She clears her throat. "Let me know when you get there, and I'll text you as soon as they airlift him. They said it should be in the next hour."

"Will do, Ness. Love you."

"Love you."

I end the call and close my eyes. After inhaling deeply, I slowly exhale, getting myself ready to start making a move. It's times like these that I envy my sister. John, her husband, is a good bloke who has her back. Right now, he'll be rallying and taking the load, hugging her hard so she doesn't have to carry the burden alone.

One day, I really hope to have that. But for now, I need to lock up the house and get on the road. I'll just visit today, then come back home. Tomorrow morning, when I know more about the recovery process and what that's going to look like, I'll start putting a plan in motion.

DAD'S SURGERY WENT WELL. WHILE I TALKED myself into it of course all being fine, getting the call from my sister after his surgery was a relief. I've visited Dad every day and have been there for some basic physio sessions.

What's clear is that the usual six weeks for a fracture is just the beginning of recovery for a hip. What that means is I've organised holiday time as well as some long-service leave, freeing me up for an additional four weeks. On top of my usual two weeks off, and with this first week off almost gone, I'll have seven weeks back in Roma.

I can take more if needed, but I hope to hell I'll be able to return to civilisation after that.

Don't get me wrong, living in the Queensland outback has its pros. For one, I had a kick-arse, free-rein childhood, but still, while the town's pretty and familiar, there's not a lot to do if you're a gay guy in your early thirties.

Roma's... well, it's "country," for want of a better word. I love the place, but I loved getting out of there too. For seven weeks, I'll survive, though. And if it keeps my dad out of mischief and gives him a good start healing, then I'll do longer if necessary.

Trev's name appears on the dash of my Cruiser,

cutting out my music. I hit Handsfree on the steering wheel. "Hey, Trev. How's it going?"

"Yeah, good, mate. You set off already to pick up your old man? He doing okay?"

I cringe as I hit another crater impossible to dodge in the road. "I expect everyone will be glad to see the back of him," I joke. The truth is, when on form, my dad can be a charmer. He's no fool either, so there's no chance he's pissing off the nurses.

The physio, however… if you believed my dad, you'd think the hospital physio is the son of Satan.

Trev chuckles. "I imagine that means he's keen to get home."

"True that. The thing is making sure he doesn't do anything stupid to mess up his healing." I'm tired already, thinking about it. It's a sobering thought.

There's no humour in Trev's voice when he says, "I bet, mate. But you know I've got your back. I'll be out there in a fortnight. Just make sure you don't start without me, yeah?"

When I cancelled on our fishing trip and Trev told me he'd head out to Roma for a couple of weeks to give me a hand, I was stoked by his offer. While he didn't grow up with cattle, he's spent a few long weekends over the years helping out. The first time was at uni when he came and met my folks. He also met Bernard, our old grumpy-arse bull, for the first time too. I swear, I've still never seen Trev move as damn fast as when the old bull took offense to being nudged.

That he's giving up his two-weeks' vacation time to give me a helping hand means a hell of a lot. "No chance of me jumping the gun if I have an extra pair of hands prepared to help me out." It's the truth. I'll manage running the day-to-day stuff, but when it comes to banding and tagging, it's at least a two-person job.

"Make that two pairs of extra hands."

I frown. "What do you mean?" I know he can't mean Charlie, since he's up north in Darwin and will be for another month.

"Alec." My heart stutters in my chest. Oblivious, Trev continues, "I told him what's going on and that I'm heading out west. When I realised he had nothing planned this Easter break, I suggested he come and give a hand. It'll give him the chance to work off those few kilos he's put on from sitting on his arse in the new admin position and grumbling about it."

My mouth goes dry. In two weeks I'll see Alec again. Fuck, I'm not prepared for that. One look at him is all it's going to take for the memory of his mouth on mine, the taste of him on my tongue to slam down on me. It's already difficult keeping thoughts of Alec at bay.

That night, for a couple of blissful hours, I thought everything had changed. The thing is, everything did change. I tasted my dream, then had it unceremoniously ripped away from me.

"Have I lost you? You still there, Pat?"

"Yeah. Just navigating traffic." The road ahead is empty. Not even a road train in sight.

"So, yeah, Alec's coming to lend another pair of hands. That's okay, right?"

"Yeah, sure." Somehow I keep the tremble out of my voice. "Did he…" I trail off, not quite sure I can ask. What I want to know is how he reacted? Was he keen? Was he bothered? Did he seem concerned about seeing me?

"Did he what?"

"Nothing," I say quickly.

Not responding straight away means Trev's thinking. A wince contorts my face. I don't think I want him to say whatever he's mulling over.

"Alec didn't hesitate to agree to help you out." Trev's no-nonsense tone is actually reassuring and settles my racing pulse.

"That's good of him." It really is. I'm not simply paying lip service.

"He has his moments." Amusement lifts his words. "If you need anything while you're there, just give me a call, yeah?"

"Will do, Trev. Thanks again."

"No worries, Pat. Safe drive."

The call ends and thoughts of Alec fill my mind. In a couple of weeks, I'll be spending a fortnight with him. It'll be fine. We'll be working most of the time anyway, and that he's fine coming to Roma has to mean he's not weirded out or anything. He may even pretend like nothing ever happened.

I rub at my chest, annoyed at the pang that is a physical ache.

Follow his lead… I can do that.

CHAPTER 5
ALEC

"You doing okay?" Ross asks as he places his coffee mug on the outside table.

There's no playing dumb here. Not that I want to. Last night's moderately overexcited, slightly terrified, and completely uncharacteristic meltdown isn't something I can ignore. Not when it was with Ross and resulted in him being here now, coffee in hand, at the arse crack of dawn.

Holding back my grin isn't possible. "I'm good. Eager to get there." It's amazing how a meltdown, a few beers, the end of a term, and kicking back with a friend can result in such an easy smile. It's genuine, though. After the last few months of reflection and discovering some interesting truths, I can't wait to get on the road.

He studies me, no doubt checking that I'm telling the truth. Since I have an abysmal poker face, it only takes a couple of seconds for his forehead to smooth out. "You're going to have a great time. Whatever happens."

I finish off my coffee, grateful he's so thoughtful. Unsurprisingly, I slept for shit last night. Today's road trip and finally seeing Patrick has me wired. "Thanks."

"And you know you can reach me, okay? With questions or whatever."

My stomach flips a little, my cheeks heating. Chuckling away my embarrassment, I say, "Like a queer hotline or something? Ross speaking, here to answer all your baby-bi *queer*ies."

Ross snorts. "Yeah, I'll be sure to answer every call from you with those exact words." He rolls his eyes, but they quickly settle back on me, knowing full well that while I'm coming out of my skin with anticipation, I'm nervous.

That Ross is invested in my sex life or at least my bi realisation is not unexpected. Especially not since I was totally on board with helping him get some action when he was single. With Dan now in his life, Ross is all about making sure I find my own slice of happy.

It's adorable really, and I don't mind it. At thirty-four, I'm far from past my prime and have enjoyed being single and getting laid a hell of a lot. Seeing Ross and Dan so loved up is nice, though. While feeling envious about a steady relationship and being in love is surprising, I'm not going to run from it. Not when I see how my best friend's world is shaping.

But it's more than that, and we both know it.

I've had a total of one encounter with a guy. The same man who I'm going to be spending two weeks with, so Ross's concern and my nerves are legit.

"I'll be fine. Trev's there. A buffer if I need one. Plus, I'm technically heading out west to lend a helping hand. There's also the whole Easter in the Country fun. I might even be able to relax. I'm not there for the sole purpose of getting laid."

When Ross's brows shoot high, I realise what I've said. My mouth goes dry.

"Hey, if you want to get laid with Patrick or anyone else, you can. It's your prerogative, yeah? No pressure from anyone."

"That night was hot," I say. "I think I'm going to be more than fine to get up close and personal with cock." While the night ended unexpectedly early, and I'll be honest, on a sour note and with a pit of unease in my stomach, the experience has not scared me off. The opposite, in fact.

Ross laughs. "You know, I'm not even surprised."

"About what, me liking D?"

"More like you attempting a threesome last December, but instead having your mind blown when a man sucked you off, and rather than you freaking, you realised you were absolutely up for it. I'm proud of you."

And fuck if mentioning being sucked off doesn't bring into stark focus an image of Patrick. Hands down, that night in Bali was the hottest night I've ever had. It's been Patrick's mouth and hands I've dreamt about. Even months later.

Ross isn't even taking the piss with his praise. For years, we've been good friends—since starting work at the same high school—and while I'm a bit full-on for a lot of people, Ross just gets me. He's never put me down or told me to curb my enthusiasm. And with my bi discovery, he's listened and encouraged me every step of the way.

I'm grateful to have him in my corner. Dan, his boyfriend, knows he's a lucky guy, and I may have added a warning a time or two about how hard I can do a footie tackle.

"Thanks, man. While I wasn't deliberately hiding this side of me or anything, fuck, I'm excited. I feel like a kid at Christmas, knowing there's a whole bunch of awesome treats to unwrap." Not necessarily this Easter. I have to keep reminding myself of that.

It's not like Patrick invited me to go. I don't even know how he reacted to my offer, beyond I'm still going so he can't have said he doesn't want me there.

"I'm sure you'll have a heap of fun, uhm… unwrapping gifts. Just make sure you wrap up, you know, if you get lucky."

A loud chuckle bursts free. "You're really giving me a safe sex talk? You know I run the HPE program and have a kick-arse scheme of work on sex ed, right?"

"Yeah, yeah." He rolls his eyes. "It never hurts to hear it again. And you know PrEP exists, right?"

Ross is being his sweet self, doing his whole intro to being a queer man thing. Legit, for my birthday last month, he bought me rainbow boxers. Not gonna lie, they made me tear up a little, and not because they were too tight on my balls.

"That I do. Maybe I'll look into it."

A text alert draws my attention away from Ross. I grin as I read it. "It's my brother. He's almost here."

With a nod, Ross stands and picks up his take-away coffee to dump in the outside bin on the way out. We pass through my house while I do a mental check that I have everything.

Last night, I made sure to pack up and get the house ready.

"You've got everything you need for the journey?" Ross eyes my duffel bag sitting next to my front door.

"Yes, Dad." I roll my eyes at him.

Rather than rise to the bait, he arches a brow, saying, "Don't you need your steel caps?"

Fuck. "I was just going to grab them." He doesn't call me out, even when I'm rummaging through my closet. The boots are covered in dust. Not surprising, since being a PE teacher doesn't tend to give me a reason to wear work boots. These things are at least ten years old, and I only got them when I was helping my folks do some home reno.

We head out the front, the autumn sun beating down on us as I lock up. Trev will be here any second, and since we have a six-hour drive ahead of us, he'll want to leave as soon as I'm strapped in.

"Give me a text letting me know you got there safely."

My lips twitch at his concern, but I also know over the past few months, there's been a whole lot of real worrying to do. Between fires and floods, Mother Nature is keeping Aussies on their toes. Instead of being an arsehole and teasing him, I nod and shake his hand, tugging him into a back-pounding hug. "You've got it." I step away and grin. "Make sure you stay away from the library and get some downtime, yeah?"

We've got two weeks off from school. I'm eager to get out of town and put some distance between me and work, needing some space from paperwork and sulky teenagers.

My new pastoral role hasn't been easy. It doesn't mean I'm not enjoying it, though.

"Will do. You make sure you don't pull your back out or anything. Gym muscles aren't the same thing as farm muscles."

I flip him off just as my brother pulls up in his car. "Don't you worry about me, arsehole." I wave at my brother and grab my bag and boots. "Catch you later, Rosco."

He waves as I greet my brother. After throwing my things in the tray and making sure they're secure, I get in the passenger seat and reach over to give my brother an awkward side hug, since his lazy arse didn't bother getting out of the car.

"You good?"

"Sure am," I answer, reaching forwards and messing with the air-con unit.

"For real? Thirty seconds and you're already fiddling."

I ignore my kid brother, sit back, and pull my phone out so I can connect it to the car's Bluetooth. This will piss him off even more. Doing so will never get boring.

"Jesus, 500 kilometres with you is going to be painful."

"You survived our flight to Bali just fine."

"And just two minutes before you mentioned Bali. A record I think." He pulls away, his grin smug as shit.

"Fuck off. I'm not that bad."

"Uh-huh."

Okay, so he's not exactly wrong. I've told every fucker who'll listen about my life-changing experience with Patrick. Even some who don't want to listen. And seriously, life-fucking-changing. Having a sexual awakening in my thirties practically blew my mind. I'm embracing it fully, keen to explore and discover this new exciting side of me.

I thought I'd known exactly who I was. Until Patrick finally got under my skin. And in my pants.

This is the first opportunity I've had to see him again. Not that we've been in contact, but it's not like we've ever just texted or called each other. I think

Trevor inviting me along for this trip is his way at shutting me up. Whether to fuck Patrick out of my system or to be disappointed by the reality of his friend not being interested, who knows.

But I kind of like the third option.

And what is that exactly?

Maybe Patrick and I can hook up and become something more. Hell, he's pursued me like a sexy country-boy hound dog over the years, one who'd got a good whiff of blood. He's flirted outrageously in fact. Ever since we first met when he came for a visit one Christmas break.

One night of blowing me and me drinking his cum can't have fulfilled all his fantasies, right? This trip, I plan to find out.

"You had a good last week at school?" my brother asks as we make it to the highway, travelling north before we turn west.

"Not too bad. Busy. Kids also needed extra reining in."

"How are the under 15s shaping up?"

I smile, thinking about the footie team I coach. "Only a few weeks in and they're tight. They're also willing to put in the work." I run a couple of extra sessions during the week, one at lunchtime with the footie lads who attend my school, and one after school. Not only do I love the game, but I have two players who are something really special.

"I'll try and take in a game."

"For sure. There's a weekend tournament coming up. I'll let you know the details." I angle to look at my brother. "So, have you talked to Patrick? Let him know when to expect us?" A bubble of excited nerves forms and pops in my gut. Jesus, I seriously hope I haven't blown our connection out of proportion.

I know it ended super clearly with the one-night-stand vibe he gave off, but still… I can't leave it alone. I need to see if there's something there.

Trevor's lips twitch, and he side-eyes me before returning his attention to the road ahead. "I have and he does."

That's it. The arsehole stares pointedly ahead.

"Seriously. Trev, stop being a shit."

He snorts. "I don't know what else you want me to say." His gaze flicks briefly to mine again. "You're here with me, right? That's my whole part done. I'm not getting involved in anything else."

While his tone is superlight, I hear the undercurrent of seriousness. I get it. This is strange for him. He took me hooking up with his friend and my bi discovery like a champ. The latter he's especially been supportive about.

"Thanks, Trev. I don't mean to make this weird for you."

He shakes his head. "Not weird, but you're my brother, he's one of my closest friends. I want you both to be happy, but I also don't want to get in the middle of anything, you know?"

"I do. I get that." I pause, staring out at the asphalt, relieved that the traffic is heading south to the Sunny Coast, rather than in our direction. I shoot him a sly look, unable to resist. "But he's got to have said something about me coming along, right?"

Since we were staying at his family's property, he would have had to give his okay at least.

Trevor rolls his eyes, reminding me a little of some of the teenagers that I teach. "He's grateful for the extra hand and the brawn you can provide."

I grin and fold my arms, twitching my pecs and flexing a little.

Trevor snorts. "Jesus, leave it for the right audience."

"He thinks I've got brawn?"

"Oh my God. I should have brought my earplugs. I swear, Alec, if this is what it's going to be like the whole journey, I'm going to lose my shit."

Chuckling, I nudge him gently. "Okay, I'll try to contain myself."

He smiles wide. "I'm glad you're excited, but just... I don't know, keep your expectations real, okay?"

His words are a punch to the gut. I part my lips, prepared to fire out questions. The shake of his head stops me.

"And no, Pat hasn't said anything to me, but Pat's never had the same guy around for longer than a month. I just want you to keep your heart safe."

I keep quiet, knowing him sharing that is more than he wanted to. He's serious about staying out of it and not being dragged into the middle of anything. From what I know about Patrick, he's fun and flirty and wears a pair of jeans really well. I also know he's always been single, works in the mining industry, and has a few acres south-west of Brisbane. Somewhere he uses more as a base since it's convenient to fly in and out to work.

He's also taking time off to spend with his dad who's injured, which is where we're heading and giving a helping hand. Two weeks on the outskirts of Roma, on a large cattle property, should be fun. Hard work, too, I expect.

Here's hoping getting to spend more time with Patrick will make the experience a whole lot more enjoyable.

CHAPTER 6

PATRICK

The water turns red before it morphs into deep brown. Tilting my head so the spray hits my achy shoulders, I groan in relief.

It's been hot as the Devil's crotch today. After he did a hundred lunges. *In* woolly sweatpants. Red dirt is wedged in every crevice. Every crease on my forehead looks like dodgy-coloured Botox has been squeezed right on in there.

"…can you believe it? Shut the fucking site down. What a dick."

"What did you expect from Murphy?" Not for the first time I wonder why I accepted Leroy's call and agreed to put the loudspeaker on while I shower. His version of an emergency is vastly overexaggerated.

What he's sharing is gossip. Pure and simple.

But as one of my mates, specifically one who has a fondness for dramatics, Leroy also keeps me sane when we're on the same job. That we're in different fields I think helps us get on even better.

"But still, the setup is a shitshow and I'm over here, expected to pull tonnes out of my arse. Talking of arses, guess who I ran into during smoko?" As expected, Leroy doesn't wait or want a response, going on to say, "Jenkins."

"Henry Jenkins?" The mention of Jenkins is enough for me to stick my head out of the spray fully so I can hear properly.

"The one and only." From Leroy's grumbly tone, he's thinking about the man's ability to be a dickhead and find fault in the most ridiculous detail. Not for the first time, I'm relieved I'm not a machine operator and have nothing really to do with site operations. Unlike Leroy.

"What was he doing on site?" As far as I know, they're not due for an inspection. "Shit, a surprise inspection?"

"Apparently not. But he was meeting with the bigwigs about something."

"Well, I'm pleased as hell I'm not there." Not that I'm involved at all. But an inspector on site causes tension.

Leroy snorts. "I seriously wish I wasn't. Shit, I have to go. Tank's calling. Make sure you try to have some fun while you're there. See ya, Pat."

He cuts off, and I shake my head, not sure where to let my thoughts settle. For one, Leroy knows I'm staying in the arsehole of the outback, so I'm not sure if fun is technically possible. Sure, the Maranoa region is beautiful in its vastness. Even the dry heat is a refreshing break from the humidity of where I spend the majority of my time on camp up north. But I'm not exaggerating the intensity of the Devil's-crotch heat.

It's autumn, for crying out loud. I sure as shit hope the cooler weather kicks in soon.

And other than picking up the slack while I'm here, I can't imagine fun being on the agenda.

I dip my head back under the steady stream, relieved Dad upgraded the water system out here, complete with solar panels, a few years back. As for work-related conversations, honestly, I don't give a shit. The reality of using my skills as a geologist compared to my dreams of the job as a kid are vastly different. Any grand visions I may have had when I finished my degree have been firmly buried with the experience of working in the mining industry.

Work is the least of my worries, though. I'm

committed to supporting Dad, so I may as well focus on washing and getting some food in me. I'm famished after being outside almost all day.

The water's turned clear, but it's going to take a good scrub to get rid of all signs of working on my old man's property. Sunscreen and red dirt do like to cling.

Despite my general grubbiness and every muscle hurting, I appreciate the ache. Life's been busy, and I haven't been out here helping my dad as often as I should. Sure, my sister and her husband have the property next door, but they also have three kids under ten, and their own lives and land to organise.

Day whatever this is of being back home, though, and I'm wondering how I managed to let myself go quite so much. Not having done hard labour—beyond the occasional week or long weekend I help Dad out —since I left home at eighteen will do that to a guy.

Getting to work at washing my arse, I focus instead on the positives—a clean butt notwithstanding.

So much time here means Dad's hip can have a good go at healing properly. There's no chance it would if I left him to his own devices. The man doesn't stop. Retirement is a concept that will never compute, either. Not that he's quite there yet.

But if he thought he could get away with it, he'd be on his tractor or hooning around on his quad or his bike in the blistering heat and wrangling the cattle if I wasn't here. The operation he had a few weeks ago would have been pointless and would probably end up needing to be redone.

If I have any say about it, that won't be happening.

I shampoo my hair, clinging to other positives.

My niblings are pretty cute, so it's been good spending time with them. I barely know Lola, which my sister reminds me of frequently. She recently turned three and is as cute as a button. If not a little feral, but in the best way.

Living a six-hour drive away isn't exactly far when we live in Queensland, but the same old excuses of work and a social life stand. Sure, it's only an hour's flight away, but yeah... excuses. But I'm here now. That's the main thing.

A few weeks of living back home is doable. Thankfully, I'm now staying in the worker's cottage and not in my old room, which is where I bunked out the first week in case Dad needed me. But leaving at eighteen to go to uni means it's been over ten years since I've stayed for longer than a week under the same roof as Dad.

We wanted to kill each other then, so there's no chance we'd cope now for longer than seven days.

Not that I don't love my dad or even get on with him.

My sister says it's because we're more similar than I'm prepared to believe.

Nessa can go and piss right off.

Anyhow, positives. What else is there?

The past couple of weeks of hard labour have already gone a long way at trimming me up. Not going to lie, since working such long hours and usually being attached to my phone, my arse planted in my work ute, rather than me heading to the gym on camp or exercising in my downtime, beer and takeouts have become my staple. That and early nights.

I could have done with losing a couple of kilos before returning. Okay, maybe closer to seven. But picking up the slack on my dad's five hundred acres has already helped me shed a few and pick up my fitness some.

There's always the relief of having a break from work too.

You've gotta love long-service leave.

Then there's hanging out with Trev when he gets here. My stomach flips over as I think about his brother, Alec. There's no stopping my thickening cock when my mind wanders back to Bali.

Hell, how I wish that night had happened at the beginning of the holiday. After the way he'd shot his load down my throat, it was clear he enjoyed it. Maybe I could have convinced him I was more than some weird bucket-list fantasy he had.

The man came alive in my arms, just like I always dreamed. Every fantasy I've had of him since I was nineteen set high expectations, and somehow, he still surpassed them all.

And now he's coming here.

Two thuds on the door followed by "Patrick," make me jolt.

"Yeah?" I call out to my dad. The front door is permanently unlatched, nothing but an unlocked flyscreen between me and the kangaroos. I turn off the shower and hear the screen door open.

Jesus, he better not have hobbled over here without support. That's probably fifty steps too many.

As I'm grabbing a towel and drying myself off, Dad shouts, "You about done?"

I close my eyes and wonder how I'm going to get through the next month. Dad grafts nonstop. He's the hardest-working man I know. Apart from pausing for thirty minutes to inhale my Vegemite-and-cheese sandwiches, this is the first time I've stopped since five thirty this morning.

He's also sort of mobile, but it's really taking it out of him.

"Yeah." It's easier than questioning him or telling him to give me a few more minutes of peace. The stubborn man avoids taking the painkillers prescribed after being released from hospital, so inevitably is still in pain. With that in mind, I expect his grouchiness. I'm just grateful he's taking the anti-inflammatories and the antibiotics.

I wrap my towel around my waist, stuff my dirty clothes in the hamper, and step out of the bathroom, rubbing my hair with a smaller towel. Stopping short when I hear a deep voice saying, "Can do," I tear my towel away—the towel I'm using to dry my hair, not the one covering my cock.

With my vision no longer obscured, my gaze settles on the man standing next to Dad. Alec. He's a couple of inches taller than my old man, who thank Christ is actually in the borrowed wheelchair we organised. Alec has the broad shoulders and tight muscles of a footie player. With a freshly shaven face, he looks even more handsome than when I last saw him, and just as hot.

And hell if my breath doesn't catch at the sight of

him. I thought I'd prepared myself to see him again, but with the way my heart thuds, apparently not.

When Alec's attention snaps to me, making eye contact, it takes me a beat to realise where his gaze previously was. From the pink crawling up his neck and settling on his cheeks, it's safe to say we both know exactly where that was.

A smile crosses his lips, and whatever embarrassment he has from being caught eyeing my half-naked form seems to pass. "Patrick, good to see you." An outstretched hand reaches for me as he takes a few steps forwards.

Okay, I can do this.

So what if the last time I saw him I was shooting my load into his mouth.

While I'm aware of Trev coming up behind him, I can't tear my eyes away from Alec. Holding my breath, I step forward and take Alec's hand.

A warm, calloused palm grips mine. His shake is firm, confident, pretty much matching the smile directed my way.

I expel a breath, some of the nerves I've been actively avoiding acknowledging, finally dissipating. "Wow, you made good time. I wasn't expecting you yet." My words are lame, and I want to wince. All my game seems to have washed down the drain. But hell,

I've been dreading this moment being uncomfortable, worried that night is one he regrets or wants to bury.

"That's what you get with a maniac behind the wheel." He's still holding my hand, our gazes unwavering. Oh how I wish my old man and Trev weren't with us right now. Greeting him with a kiss wouldn't be too weird, right?

"Just because I know how to drive and dodge potholes and roos without getting side-swiped doesn't make me a maniac."

We both startle, our hands releasing when Trev speaks.

I chuckle and side-step Alec as Trev makes his way forwards. I clasp his hand and hug him. "I think your brother's got it right."

Smiling, Trev steps back. "Good to see you, Pat. Good of you to dress for the occasion."

Heat sweeps across my cheeks, and I'm not sure who's more surprised, me or Trev. I don't embarrass easily, but with Alec being within touching distance, and next to my dad, plus knowing Trev's got a good idea of what went down between me and his big brother, heck, I need to get some clothes on before I unravel.

"It's great to have you both here." I turn back to Alec, roaming his features.

My smile is genuine as I take him in, appreciating how easy on the eyes he is and how his gaze shifts to my chest. He catches himself, quicker this time, focus snapping up to make eye contact once again. A small smirk follows, and I like it a lot.

He really is smoking hot and has this whole sun-kissed, beefy, muscly jock thing going on.

Before I can say anything else, Dad says, "You want to put some snags on… after you've put clothes on." He rolls his eyes at me. "I'll put the barbie on."

I fight back my blush from still standing here in a towel, becoming super aware my dick's free underneath the grey bath sheet. "Right." I chuckle. "I best get dressed. I'll then get a beer in your hand."

Somehow I manage to pull my attention from Alec and his deep brown eyes. I need to focus on dressing and toning down my desire to pounce on the man. It's been months since I laid eyes on him, so I don't even know where his head's at. Plus, I don't want to be in Trev's face about just how much of a hard-on I have for his brother.

Sure, I've been full-on with my flirting game in the past, but this feels different. *Then* I didn't think I had a shot. Now? Well, we have two weeks to find out. Maybe I can get him to rethink his bucket list.

CHAPTER 7

ALEC

Having a barbeque is an Aussie staple. Every man from here to Adelaide to Perth and back again will have had so many. I reckon there'd be plenty of rich Aussies out there if they got a dollar a barbie.

This one right here, with Patrick turning the snags and flipping the burgers, all while doing his utmost to not hold my gaze, is going to be one that won't fizzle in my memories.

And why's that exactly? The blushes I've never seen on him before, for starters. The pink spreading on his cheeks every time our gazes catch is impossible to ignore or look away from. And the way he smells. Holy shit, when he stepped out his bathroom earlier, bringing with him the scent of shampoo and what I'm sure is tea tree shower gel, I'd all but swallowed my tongue. But since he dressed and I stood close to him when he passed me a beer, that fresh scent mingles with the one still etched into my memory.

It's masculine, a mix of body spray and Patrick. The scent assaulted my memories, and I popped a boner in two point five seconds. Yeah, shuffling back to my seat with no one noticing took some smooth moves.

Patrick laughs loudly at his dad, Graham. And it's the first time in the past hour I've seen him truly at ease. It's this version I recognise. Witty, fun, and outgoing. Sure, he can be a grumbly shit like the rest of us, but I'll take that rather than the version that casts nervous glances my way.

"Screw off, old man." Patrick follows up with a deep chuckle and a shake of his head. "My scream was not *that* loud."

Graham guffaws. "Bloody oath you were." He glances at me and winks. "If you'd heard him, Alec, you'd have thought he'd come face-to-face with an eight-foot croc, not a piddly little snake." He continues to crack up. "Loud enough to wake the dead and cause a quake, I reckon."

"Well, there's something to be said about a man who's not afraid to scream." My eyes widen as soon as I spill the words. There's clear flirtation and innuendo there, and his dad's sitting just a few metres from me. My face heats, Trev snorts loudly, but it's Patrick choking on his beer that grabs my attention.

"Uhm." I've seriously got nothing. There's no save from that. I dart a quick look at his dad. His brow's quirked, his lips pulled between his teeth in a thin line. Yeah, he looks like he's close to laughing his arse off.

Patrick wipes his mouth and clears his throat, drawing my attention back to him. "Damn straight I screamed. It was a brown snake that practically launched itself at me." He winks at me, and I pull in a breath, grateful for him coming to my aid. "I reckon the time you went head-to-head with that wild boar beat the volume of my scream, Dad. Wake the dead?" He snorts and points at his dad. "It was almost enough to start a zombie apocalypse. Especially when you landed arse over tit in the dam."

We all chuckle as Graham flips off his son. "Bloody cold that dam was. In the middle of winter when that boar came out of nowhere. No way was I letting it gut our old dog Lucky."

"Snakes and boars." I grin, relaxing into the banter. "Are these your 'welcome to the outback' tales?" My gaze travels to Patrick.

"Just be grateful we're not further north so we don't have crocs." Another wink follows, and my stomach flips. I smirk in response, my attention moving to Trev when he stands and heads over to Patrick, no doubt smelling the meat's cooked.

As he helps plate it up, I turn to Graham. I've only met the man once before, and that was at Trev and Patrick's graduation. Considering he had an operation about three weeks ago, he looks remarkably well. Sure, he's slow on his feet and, as much as I'm sure he tries to hide it, in pain, but despite all that, he seems fit and healthy.

"And how's it been having Patrick home?"

Graham takes a swig of his tin of beer before saying, "The kid's a pain in my arse and on my case, but he's a good kid."

"Trying to keep you out of mischief is hard work." Patrick places a plate of burgers in the middle of the table, then sits down opposite me on the picnic bench.

"Give over. I'm not that bad," Graham grumbles and rolls his eyes before shooting me a conspiratorial wink.

I grin. The gesture is so similar to his son's that it warms me up to the man even more. It's obvious where Patrick got his wise-arse mouth from.

Trev sits next to me, setting down the plate of snags. "You'll have to give Pat some discipline techniques that you use at school on misbehaving kids," he says with a chuckle.

"Not sure anything that works on seventeen-year-olds will work on you, Graham."

"I don't know," Patricks says before his dad can respond. "I can think of a few choice lines Dad could do with writing out."

"Yeah, like 'do a better job at teaching your kids how to respect their elders.'"

We all laugh and dig into the food. It's been a long day of travelling, and I've eaten too much junk food. While snags and burgers aren't exactly healthy, I make sure I have a decent-sized salad on my plate.

As we eat, Patrick tells us what he's been doing on the property since he arrived and explains what we're going to be doing the next few days. The more he talks, the more at ease I become, and I think he does too.

The tension around his eyes, impossible to ignore earlier, has faded away. His smiles are quick and his laughter natural. On the wraparound veranda of his dad's house, the cooling night air brushing over our skin, pushing away the heat of the afternoon sun, I relax and savour each deep laugh. But it's when

Patrick's not as fast to pull his gaze away from mine that has my chest feeling lighter.

By the time it's pitch-black and the temperature has dropped, Graham's already turned in, and Patrick walks me and Trev back over to where we first met him this afternoon.

"Where do you want us?" Trev asks.

It's oh so tempting to make a suggestion about sharing a bed with Patrick, but I'm jumping the gun and getting way ahead of myself. Every time he's smiled at me over the past few hours, it's been easier to forget how he ran out as soon as he got off. But I mustn't ignore the reality of how we left things.

"I've set myself up in the two-bedroom worker's cottage," he says when we step onto the small porch. He turns to us. "Which now I think about it, I should have left for you guys. I just wanted the better shower, to be honest."

"We can share, or do you have a sofa bed or something?" Trevor asks.

"There's actually a donga just behind this place. One bed, small kitchenette, sofa, and an en suite with a shower. I can move my stuff out, so you guys can have—"

"Don't be daft, mate." My brother shakes his head. "You're already set up. I can take the donga.

Alec here's used to a little more luxury than a box of a mobile home. Not sure how he'd fair in a donga."

I should be flipping him off, but instead I could kiss him. Whatever his aim, that he's letting me share the same space as Patrick is great. "Yeah, sounds good," I say, not biting, and not quite curbing my enthusiasm.

Trevor snorts. "Thought so." He looks at Patrick. "Just behind this place?"

"Yeah." Patrick nods a little stiffly. "It's all connected to the power."

"Sounds good. What time are we up in the morning?"

"There's nothing too crazy on tomorrow. We can take it easy and show Alec around." He glances at me, and I smile gratefully. "We need to move the cattle to a new paddock, ready for Tuesday. Yarran's going to head out to help us."

"Yarran as in…?" my brother says cryptically. I notice Patrick's nod and look between the two of them.

"Yarran as in who?" I ask, rarely one to beat around the bush.

Patrick answers after he shoots Trevor a death glare. "Just a friend who lives in town. Said he'd stop by and help out when he could. It's Sunday tomorrow, so he said he'll come by after church."

Surprise slams into me. Church? Hell, I don't know a single person who goes to church these days. I keep my mouth shut and simply nod.

"I thought tomorrow arvo, we could head into Roma. There's not much open on Sunday, though."

Trevor chuckles. "Is there anything but the pub open on a Sunday?"

"Woolies now opens. Ten years back, you would have been out of luck wanting to head to the supermarket."

"Seriously? The supermarket didn't used to open on a Sunday?" I shake my head. "Was it like growing up in the seventies, you reckon?" I tease.

Patrick snorts. "Something like that. I swear there are times it still feels that way."

"It's got a charm to it, though, right?" Trev says, stepping back towards where we've parked. I'm assuming to grab his bag. "I always liked the town. There's a quaintness to it. Felt like there was a real community here."

I follow Trevor's lead and go and grab my bag and boots.

"From the lasagnes, stews, batch of lamingtons,

and pumpkin scones sitting in the freezer, I can confirm the community's going strong."

Pausing, I peer back to see if Patrick's teasing. He's smiling, but I don't think he's bullshitting. "That food is what… care packages or something?"

He nods. "Exactly that. Folks heard about Dad's accident, and the food started pouring in." He gazes around the dark yard. With the only lights coming from the porch and the distant outdoor lighting of the main house, the place seems extra peaceful.

It's also incredibly dark. Seriously. It's been a long time since I've experienced such absolute inky blackness when outside. One of the pitfalls of living in a hinterland town that's a stone's throw from the busy coast.

But Patrick, with nothing but the faint glow of lights that flicker with the shadows from kamikaze moths, and the millions of stars overhead, looks content here. This place fits him. He's bitched off his hometown a few times over the years, but now I think about it, it was things like the challenge of being a gay kid in a small town, and not necessarily about locals being arseholes, but more about there was no one really to hook up with. That and something about a one-screen cinema that's since been shut down.

"It has its benefits, living in such a small community, I bet." Our gazes connect and he bobs his head in response.

"You sure you're good with the sleeping arrangements?" I ask Trevor. It's the polite thing to ask, right?

He flicks his attention to me as he closes the tailgate. A smirk twitches his lips. "Yeah. I'm good. Don't worry about me." He switches on a torch I assume he pulled out of his ute and calls out goodnight to us before he makes his way around the side of the small cottage.

The sounds of his footsteps fade away, the quiet quickly encroaching until all I hear are the occasional cows bellowing in the distance and the sounds of insects rubbing their legs or fluttering their wings, or whatever the noisy creatures do.

I glance up at the sky. It only takes a moment for my vision to adjust. No lie, skies like these take my breath away. Too many stars to count fill my vision. Some in clusters, some in clear formations that even I can recognise.

The crunch of dirt under shoes alerts me to Patrick moving. While I'm tempted to focus on him, I'm reluctant to pull my attention away from the constellations above me. Patrick stops beside me. The sound of his gentle breathing is comforting. Not quite familiar, but a flash of memory of heavy, heated breaths is difficult to ignore.

"It's beautiful out here." My voice is low, barely a whisper. It feels wrong to speak loudly.

"It is. If you look right there"—he points up and angles us around—"we can see Mars."

It takes a beat to follow his line of sight, but I see the planet clearly. It's a fair size bigger than the pinprick of stars surrounding it. There's also a slight halo of colour around it. "It's incredible, right?" I marvel as he drops his arm. "That we can see something that's so far away. Makes me feel insignificant."

"Not sure you could ever be insignificant."

His words catch me by surprise. I jerk my gaze to him, eyes widening at his proximity.

How I didn't see him before, like *really* see how gorgeous he is, how I didn't open up to the possibility of being with Patrick sooner, makes me want to nut punch myself. It's not like his flirting has ever been subtle.

How the fuck could I have spent so many years brushing his attention aside?

While his face is tilted to the sky, I'm sure he's aware of my movements. Aware I'm all but gawping at him.

"What do you see when you look up?" It's the

only thing I can think to ask, too tongue-tied and feeling a little out of my depth.

We're silent for a while as we both stare up. The nocturnal insects continue their serenade, and the barely there moon emits a comforting glow. Finally, Patrick says, "Possibility."

Goosebumps travel along my arms at that one word. Is he saying that because I'm here? Does he feel something… anything from seeing me again?

The questions are on the tip of my tongue, but I bite them back. It doesn't feel like the time.

While I have just two weeks in the outback, I absolutely don't want to leave anything till the last night. Not again. Nor do I want another one-night stand. The certainty of that thought hits me hard.

Patrick isn't any random guy I want to explore my sexuality with. Trevor's words about Patrick not really dating buzz in my brain, but he could say the exact same thing about me. Hell, he may have done with Patrick.

No. With talk of possibility and of not being insignificant, I want to see if the connection between us is more than the spark that dances over my skin when he's near.

We're compatible in the sack. Well, I'm up for

handjobs and bjs for sure. The rest makes my dick harden at the thought. So that's something.

"I'm going to head in and get some shuteye. You staying out here a while?"

I shake my head. "No, I'll head in too. If you're going to put me through my paces, I expect I'll need a good night's sleep." We make eye contact and I smirk.

Patrick's lips twitch. "Based on my fortnight of getting my arse kicked by red dirt, barbed wire, and the sun, not sure I'm the one who'll be cracking a whip."

"Isn't being a cowboy like riding a bike?" I joke as we head back to the cottage.

"Ha. You see any horses around here?"

"No, thank God," I reply with a laugh. "Don't get me wrong, they're beautiful creatures, but temperamental as fuck. Am I right?"

At my side, Patrick snorts. "That you are. My sister's horse when we were kids almost took a chunk out of my hand once. Bastard thing. Fortunately, Dad would ride a bull over a horse any day of the week." He opens the flyscreen door and holds it for me.

My heart does a ridiculous flip at the gesture. "A bull?" I shake my head. "You know what, I can imagine Graham doing a bit of bull riding in his time."

We pause inside, and I place my boots near the door. "No bull-riding talk while you're here. Don't want to give the old man ideas." He reaches into the fridge and pulls out two bottles of water. "Here." He passes me a cold bottle. "The water's safe from the taps. It's tank water. The stuff at the main house tastes like shit, though. Bore water. Town's on bore water too. It's worse than the stuff out here."

"For real?" I'm far enough out of the bigger suburbs of the city to rely on rain-tank water at my place. In my opinion, it's the best type of water going. But bore water? I wrinkle my nose, earning me a chuckle.

"Careful, your city's showing."

I roll my eyes. "I'm not that bad. I've gotta be honest, though. Drinking bore water isn't on my list of things to do."

There's a flicker of something on his face that I can't quite read. Shit, have I offended him? I don't think I have, since he's the one who said the water tastes like crap.

The two deep lines that appeared between his eyebrows smooth out, and a tight smile forms.

"Right," he says, with the barest shake of his head as he glances away. "So bathroom's here."

"I remember," I say. Heat fills my cheeks at not only the memory of Patrick being wrapped in a towel, but at how breathy I sound. I subtly clear my throat. "And my room?"

The briefest of looks my way lets me know he heard me loud and clear. Rather than calling me out on it, he steps towards a closed door and opens it. "This is yours. I'm next door."

Bloody hell. Here's hoping the walls are thick; I'm not sure how I'll cope hearing Patrick rustling his sheets.

I wonder if he sleeps naked.

"Up for breakfast by seven, okay?"

I bob my head, pushing my thoughts aside. "No worries."

"Enjoy the lie-in."

Hearing the amusement in his voice, I chuckle, relieved he's no longer frowning. "Cheers for that." I glance at him, and our gazes catch. "Night, Patrick." I give him an up nod and disappear into my room. It's too risky not to. Making a fool of myself is too easy.

I close the door and peer around the tidy room. The cotton sheets are navy, suiting the off-white walls. There's a built-in wardrobe, a chest of drawers, and bedside cabinets either side of the double bed.

At home, I'm spoiled with a king, but a double will do me just fine.

A jaw-cracking yawn escapes as I place my bag on the chest of drawers. Being in a car for so long makes for a killer of a day, and I wasn't even the one driving. I bet Trevor's already fast asleep.

I set about getting my toiletries and phone charger out of my bag. It's about all I can manage before I finally collapse in bed. As I zone out, letting sleep take me, I smile into the darkness.

Visiting here feels like the right decision. Even if when I leave it's with nothing happening between Patrick and me, I can do so knowing we've cut through the awkwardness. It took a little bit of warming up between us tonight, but I think we'll be just fine.

CHAPTER 8

PATRICK

With the midday sun spilling on Alec's face as he laughs loudly, I don't think he's ever looked more beautiful.

"You might want to…" Trev trails off with a nudge. When I glance at him, he wipes the corner of his mouth, adding, "You've got a little something…"

"Fuck off." I shove him, but of course he barely budges. Another deep laugh booms, snagging my attention immediately. Yes, I'm totally staring, but how can I not when Alec is so in his element, holding court and looking so happy.

A giggling Lola is wedged under his arm while he chases after the soccer ball. Archie is hot on his heels, but rather than calling Alec out at his obvious cheating, my six-year-old nephew is grinning wildly. Even

Sienna's in on the game. My surly niece who behaves far too much like a fifteen-year-old rather than the nine-year-old she is hollers out shit talk. Fortunately of the PG variety so she doesn't get in trouble with her mum.

"I don't know how he does it," I admit, my gaze not straying from my niblings having fun with the man of my dreams. Super sappy, I know, but there are only so many times I can kid myself into believing otherwise.

Even after yesterday's reminder of his check list, today has proven that.

We started the day with an easy breakfast filled with banter and smiles, then followed up with a tour of the property in the side by side. It's been lowkey with not a lick of awkwardness.

My sister and niblings showed up with lunch. Just Vegemite-and-cheese sangas. They hit the spot and sorted us for the only real work we need to do in a little while—move the cattle ready for inoculations. Fortunately, it's just two paddocks over, but there are some skittish heifers in the herd, and a few steers who like to think they're boss.

"Does what?" Trev asks, tugging me from my thoughts.

"The whole teaching thing. I bet he's good at it,

though." While my niblings are a different age group than the high schoolers he teaches, he's super comfortable and seems to be having fun keeping them entertained.

"He's enjoying the pastoral position he took on. I'm not surprised he got the promotion."

I bob my head, recalling Alec telling me when we were in Bali about the deputy head of house role he was starting in January. "I bet," I agree. The high school I attended had a house system, and it was Mr Sorenson and Miss Jewels who were super invested and looked out for us. They were our house leaders, and did everything from boosting house spirit, to checking on welfare and making sure we toed the line.

The thing I remember the most is their office door was always open, and Miss Jewels especially went above and beyond to help her students out. I imagine Alec being the same.

"The kids are lucky to have him. I bet he's busy, though."

Trev shrugs. "I think he got a class taken off him or something, but generally with all the extracurricular stuff he has to do for PE, he's usually full-on busy. He doesn't really complain."

A plume of dust catches our attention before the

sound reaches us. A familiar ute is heading our way. Yarran. Immediately, Trev chuckles.

"What?" I fold my arms, aiming for nonchalance. The twist in my gut still happens, though.

"Was Yarran coming your idea?"

I huff out a breath, shoulders sagging. "No, but he means well. I saw him last week. Not like that," I quickly add when Trev looks my way with raised brows. "I was in town, and he saw me. Said he'd stop by and give me a hand this weekend when I gave him my plans. I told him I had friends heading over, but he said he was happy to come."

"I just bet he did." The arsehole's lips twitch.

As Yarran's ute gets closer, my stomach sinks that little bit more.

Yarran is a guy I've hooked up with a few times over the years when I've visited home. Admittedly, it's been maybe two years since the last time, but not for his lack of trying. And I get it. There are slim pickings around for sure, but while Yarran's perfect for a good conversation and is a fun lay, I just wasn't feeling the latter anymore. Shit to admit, especially because he's such a nice guy.

But because he's Yarran and is a genuine bloke, he keeps taking my rejection in his stride. That doesn't mean he's stopped offering to keep me entertained when I'm local. And while he smiles and says it's okay, the looks of longing he shoots my way make me feel rotten.

And fuck if it doesn't remind me of this situation I'm in with Alec. I swallow hard. Is feeling uncomfortable what Alec experienced all the times I've flirted with him over the years? Jesus, I hope not. I have to believe he didn't. It was a whole different situation with me flirting but never asking him out or actually coming on to him, right?

Alec's never had to say no or turn me down, as I never asked for anything from him.

Yarran pulls up, which gets the kids' attention and Alec's.

"This should be good."

"Not helping," I hiss to Trev. He's met Yarran a few times, knows our history, and knows he's keen for more.

Not for the first time, I feel shit that he won't give up. I don't think I've led him on, but that he still showed up for me suggests otherwise. Hell, it's probably just because he's a better man than I am.

"G'day," Yarran hollers as soon as he steps out of the car. His smile is bright, teeth gleaming next to his dark skin.

Archie immediately races up to him. "Hey, Coach.

We've just been having a game of soccer with Alec. He's really good."

Yarran smiles down at Archie and ruffles his hair. "That right? Sounds fun." He peers over at Alec in interest, his eyes lingering, which I totally get. I find it hard to pull my attention away all the time. That doesn't mean I have to like it.

"Hey, Yarran." I step forwards to greet him. Am I trying to pull his focus away so he stops eye fucking Alec? For sure. It's been hard enough over the years watching the gaggle of women throwing themselves at him. I don't want to witness men doing it too. Especially not since I know what his come face looks like. "Thanks for coming." I reach out and shake Yarran's hand, my smile genuine. I'm not that much of a dickhead.

While it doesn't sound like it, I like hanging out with Yarran. He's good company. He also coaches a couple of the kids' NRL teams in town. What else is there to know about Yarran? He's handsome, with deep brown eyes and a medium-brown skin tone. His shoulder-length hair suits him. And his smile is always warm and friendly.

Yarran also happens to be a history teacher at the private high school in town. Which I realise with dread is something else he'll have plenty to talk about with Alec. Being jealous isn't a fun trait, so I try hard to bury the emotion.

With a friendly smile aimed my way, Yarran shakes my hand as my nephew darts away. "No worries. After church, I met with the elders to finalise plans for the float for next weekend. It's why I'm a little late."

Trev joins us, as does Alec.

"Good to see you again, Yarran." Trev shakes his hand. "This is my brother, Alec."

I clench my jaw and shoot Trev the stink eye. There was too much glee in that introduction.

"G'day." Alec smiles warmly, and I find it hard to look away as he shakes Yarran's hand.

"G'day. It's good that Pat here has so many willing hands. Not sure he's used to so much hard work these days."

I roll my eyes. "Geez, I'm not that bad. Every year I come and help."

"Uh-huh. This time we get to keep you for seven whole weeks." Yarran smirks at me. I shake my head at him, gaze travelling to Alec, who's studying Yarran intently.

"So," I say quickly, feeling the need to steer the conversation, "next week and Easter in the Country. You all prepared?"

"Sure am. Well, as much as I can be when I'm juggling my time between two floats. It'll be good, though. The kids at school are showcasing their upcoming musical, so I've been able to take a step back a little, and the drama and art departments are taking the lead. I'm working with the SAC, you know, the Aboriginal Corp in Surat, for their parade float. We're going all in this year with a heap of the Indigenous community involved."

"That sounds great."

"You going to be coming along?" he asks me and then looks at Trev and Alec. "You guys ever taken in an Easter in the Country before?"

They both shake their heads.

"Not yet," Alec says. "Heard about it, though. It gets busy, right?"

"It sure does," Yarran answers. "Easter and the Roma Cup are the two big events that bring in tourists and the locals. Easter is the best, though, for sure. There's a real sense of community. There's loads planned too. Plus the rodeo's in town, and the live music is usually great."

"Sounds good." Alec looks at me. "It all depends on what our boss here says. Not sure what he has planned for us all while we're here." There's a definite hint of flirtation in his tone. It settles something

deep in my chest, knowing we haven't lost this cama-
raderie.

"I reckon we'll be able to take some time out, go and experience some of the local festivities." Our gazes remain connected as I smile.

"This rodeo have some of that bull riding you were talking about yesterday?" He quirks a brow.

"For sure." Teasing fills my tone. "Nothing like seeing cowboys in arse-hugging jeans and their thighs working."

"Jesus." Trev cuts in with a shove. "And I think it's time to get to work." He rolls his eyes, but amusement rolls off him.

That's our cue, and even though I'm a little on edge with both Yarran and Alec around me, we get to work.

With eighty-two cows to round up and nudge, it takes some wrangling. But with Yarran on Dad's dirt bike, me on the quad, and Trev and Alec in the side by side, with Alec jumping out every now and then to open and close gates, we get it done with only a couple of hiccups and more laughter than I expected.

Once the gate is latched, the four of us lean over the metal railing. The temperature's cooled, making it more pleasant, and despite the dust from the running cattle, there's no breeze. Not even a gum leaf stirs.

The land's flat here, making the sky so big, we can see way into the distance for kilometres. I love the emptiness, the peace, and I can't help wondering what Alec thinks. Does he think there's too much space, too much distance between where we are and civilisation?

While it was the distance that had me leaving so many years ago, now I see the long grasses painting the ground in greens and yellows and believe it's one of the most idyllic sights I've ever seen.

I really do miss this place. It's effortless being here. But with Alec at my side, feeling his presence so acutely, I can't help but wonder if part of the rightness is because he's here with me.

After a few more moments of absorbing the expanse and expelling a content breath, I smile. "I think beers are in order," I say, relieved this one job's over. The big job on Tuesday is close, but it's good to start ticking items off the list.

Alec's next to me, one of my old Akubras on his head and a smile on his face when he glances at me. I return it immediately, taking in the red dust on his cheeks and his sweaty brow. There's a satisfied sparkle in his gaze that I recognise as a job well done.

I get it. Feel it.

At eighteen I was eager to get out of here, but

there's something to be said for open space, red dirt, and aching limbs. Especially when the latter is from farm work.

"How's your arse?" I ask him, grinning wildly at the memory of him landing on his butt when he leapt out of the not quite still ATV, trying to shut the gate on a skittish weaner. When it happened, my breath stilled in my lungs, but only for the barest of seconds. In no time at all, he was up and racing to the gate, hat forgotten, and leaving a trail of cloudy dirt behind him.

"A bit of a pinch. Nothing I can't handle." Amusement colours his words, and I'd like to think I know him well enough that he's teasing.

"Well, if you need help rubbing in some arnica or something, you know where I am."

His brows shoot high, and I freeze at the surprise on his features. Have I overstepped again?

I should apologise, perhaps take it back, but Yarran, who's standing on the other side of Trev, calls out, "Town for a few beers?"

With my gaze now on Yarran, I bob my head. "Sounds good. Beers are on me, though."

"Even better. Looks like I'll be stumbling home, then." He chortles and claps Trev on the back. "Am I right to wash up here? Make use of that awesome shower you have in the cottage?"

The muscles in Alec's forearms tense. He has them balancing on the gate, so it's impossible to miss.

"Yeah, sure. Have at it," I respond as nonchalantly as possible, sure as hell Alec's wondering why he's so familiar with the high-pressure shower. I avoid Alec's gaze. It's ridiculous, I know. Me and Yarran hooking up over the years isn't a secret, and it's certainly nothing I regret. But with Alec beside me, and the memory of the taste of his cum at the front of my mind, I have to admit, I don't want him to feel threatened or uncertain or some shit.

Fuck, I seriously need to get over myself.

Bucket list.

The thought is what I need to help me rein in any fanciful ideas I may have.

"Thanks." Yarran arches his brow. "There's always room for one more. A nice big shower like that."

And there it is. The words I was hoping Yarran wouldn't share. I close my eyes, only to reopen and peer over at him. The fuck? Yarran's gaze is not on me. He's fixed on Alec, whose face is flushed as he seems to be staring hard into the distance.

"Everywhere we go." Trev's amused voice cuts

through my pissed-off haze. "I have to ask, is gaydar or bi-dar… or whatever really a thing?" Shaking his head, Trev removes his hat and sweeps his hand through his sweat-soaked hair.

I watch the movement, but my brain is 100 percent on the "bi-dar" comment. *Bi.* Air catches in my throat, the sound strangled.

Is Alec bisexual?

My gaze snaps to him as I drag in a breath. He's looking at me, this time with concern. No doubt wondering what the fuck my deal is.

"You okay?"

I nod a little numbly, desperate to ask if he's actually bi, right along with a million other questions.

"It seriously is," Yarran says, completely oblivious to how Trev's words have rocked my world. "But it's a talent. You, you hunk of deliciousness, are, alas, so not willing to play for the sexy team of cock."

I roll my eyes that Yarran is in full-on flirt mode. I'd argue he's worse than me… or better, depending on your perspective. Not that I've had much game since December.

Alec snorts loudly at my side. He's glorious as he tilts his head back and laughs loudly. All too soon, he angles away to look at his brother and Yarran. "Sexy team of cock?" He bobs his head. "I like it. Has a certain ring to it."

"That it does. One that, if I'm not mistaken, suits you quite well." The lightness of his tone is teasing and filled with enough humour to leave Alec an opening to say rack off if he wants to.

Holding my breath around Alec so often is going to result in me passing out if I'm not careful.

"Not sure if I should be taking that as a compliment or not." He's still facing away, but I'm sure he's smiling.

With a wide grin and a quirked brow, Yarran nods. "Definitely a compliment. Right." He claps his hands. "Let's wash up and get some beers down our necks."

We step away from the fence and make it back to the vehicles. Before Alec and Trev step into the side by side, Yarran calls out, "You can ride with me if you want, Alec. You said you'd yet to ride on a bike. No safer perch than right here." He taps the section of the seat that's behind him.

It's such a small space, Yarran would have to be all but sitting on Alec's lap to make it work. Like hell is that happening.

"No way." My words get three pairs of eyes fixed on me. I focus on Yarran. "There's not a spare helmet."

Yarran pinches his lips, clearly holding back his laughter. "I'll go slow. He'll be right."

My gaze narrows that the arsehole is calling me out. "The seat on Dad's bike isn't really made for two blokes." Internally I'm rolling my eyes at myself, but I'm in this now. I release a heavy breath and look at Alec.

He's openly staring at me, his head tilted slightly. I like the idea of him getting his fill, but I'm an idiot if I believe that's why he's looking at me.

"If you want to go out on a bike, I'll teach you how another time. I've still got my old Yamaha in the shed. We can go out together." Yarran's snort isn't subtle, and Trev's sigh is far from quiet. "With helmets," I tag on.

Yeah, nothing to see here. It's just me doing the safe, responsible thing.

"There enough room on the back of the quad?" If I thought Alec looked wired and happy with a dirty face after mustering, right here, his shoulders lifting a little in eagerness, he looks ecstatic.

"Yeah. There's enough room." And he'll absolutely need to hold on to me.

"Doesn't he need a helmet for—"

"He'll be fine. He can wear mine, and we'll go slow." I cut my gaze at Yarran, shooting him a promise of retaliation. Even as I do, I relax, relieved Yarran is teasing, and I expect reading me like a damn horny book.

Showing me his palm, he angles away. "No problem. Just making the suggestion, is all."

"And if that's all settled, are we good to go?" Apparently Trev's over my ridiculousness.

"Yeah. Just remember the gate rule."

He gives me a thumbs-up, starts the engine, and shoots off. A beat later, the dirt bike takes off after him.

"You ready?" I pass Alec the helmet from the quad.

A few steps and he's in my space. "You sure you don't need it?"

"Nah. I'm good. You're prettier than me, so are worth protecting." When his cheeks heat, I wink and straddle the seat of the quad. Earning his blushes is familiar territory. I've had years of practice at it.

The large hand of his that I recollect has callouses, which added extra friction when he explored my skin, lands on my shoulder. A movement presses him up against me.

I calm my breathing. "You're good to hold on."

There's no hesitation as he wraps his arms around me, and I'm wishing I hadn't insisted on the helmet.

Though, focusing on missing the dips and bumps would be a test of my concentration if I felt his soft breaths against my neck.

"You okay?"

"Definitely." With joy evident in that one word, I smile, start the engine, and head in the direction of the shed, lapping up every loud laugh and tight squeeze Alec gifts me.

CHAPTER 9

ALEC

Today's been a blast. Rounding up and steering cattle got my blood pumping. It feels like a bonus that I had such good fun while hanging out with my brother, Patrick, and Yarran.

While I haven't been able to as much lately, with my new position, I normally spend a lot of time outdoors for my job. Out on the property, it's different, though. Under the bright sun with no sign of a cloud in the sky, the space around me felt limitless.

"The skies are so big here."

My brother looks at me like I've had too many beers, but Patrick's bobbing his head. "I hear you. It feels that way, especially when the blue isn't smudged by white clouds. It feels like you can see the curvature of the world."

"Yes, that." I point at him, happy he gets it.

"You should see it at night," Yarran adds. "The vastness is incredible."

I nod. "Yeah, last night before bed, I noticed how many stars were visible."

Yarran shakes his head while I'm talking. "Nah, mate. You need to keep heading out west. There's an observatory out in Charleville, but there's a couple of great local spots, perfect for taking a swag and soaking in the cosmos." He sips at his beer, still focussed on me. He turns his attention to Patrick. "You should take Alec out there for the night."

My heart stutters in my chest, liking the sound of that a hell of a lot. "That would be awesome. Do we have time for that?" My gaze moves to Patrick. Openly staring at me, he doesn't glance away when our eyes connect. "How far is it?"

He swallows before saying, "Just under three hours. That something you'd like to do?"

I'm already nodding enthusiastically. "Heck yes. You got a spare swag?"

"Dad's got one you can use."

I grin. It's been years since I camped out under the stars. These days any semblance of camping I do is on school trips.

"Usually I'd question whether I was invisible,"

Trev says with absolutely zero bite, "but if you guys want to camp out, have at it. I'll gladly kick back with Graham and a few beers."

I sit a little higher on my stool, eager to spend some time with Patrick, and under the stars to boot. That's romantic as fuck, right? Almost date territory, surely. "Excellent, thanks, Trev." Looking over at Patrick, I can't hold back my excited grin. "So when are we going to do this? When do we have time around what needs to be done?"

He rubs the back of his neck, clearly thinking. "This coming weekend is Easter, so we have the events in town. You want to go, yeah?"

"Yeah, definitely."

"Perhaps this Thursday, before the tourists swarm the place on Good Friday."

"Will that give us enough time to work the cows?"

Patrick's lips twitch. "Work the cows, huh?" I roll my eyes, and he continues, "Should be fine to finish up by Thursday midday. We'll start Tuesday morning getting the cows vaccinated and sprayed. There's some bull calves that need banding too, and some need tagging."

"Sounds like a plan."

"And what's on the cards tomorrow?" Trev asks.

"There's a paddock that needs baling. I can teach one of you guys how to do that. I have to take Dad for physio at nine. It's just for an hour and in town. I need to do a general check of the fence perimeter, something that's done every Monday. I also need to look at one of the dam pumps. It's not working right. The fence lines need poisoning too. It's a big job so will need more than a day, but I'd like to at least get around the main house done."

I don't know how his dad manages it all. Everything sounds more than a one-person job.

"Just tell us where you need us, and we'll make a good start on the list," I say, determined to get as much done as possible to make his life easier.

"How about I come by and pick up Graham for his physio?" Yarran offers.

He seems like a good guy, even though I'm sure he has some history with Patrick. The thought sours my stomach, but I don't let it fester. How can I when he suggested I have a night alone with Patrick? If something has happened between them in the past, I don't think they're anything but friends now. While I want to know more, it's not something I can blurt out and ask.

"You don't mind?" Patrick asks.

"Course not. I have a couple of jobs to do in town anyway. I'll come by at eight thirty to collect him."

Gratitude morphs Patrick's features, and I'm just as grateful that Yarran has lightened the load. "I owe you one." Patrick lifts his beer in salute.

Yarran chuckles deeply. "And I'll definitely collect."

I freeze, beer to my mouth, and my eyes widen at the outright flirtation and promise in Yarran's voice. It's Patrick who splutters on his beer, though. His face is red and he's smacking on his chest. Watery-eyed from choking, he stares at Yarran and flicks a nervous glance at me.

That has to mean something. That look my way to check on my reaction. My dating history isn't much better than Patrick's, if I'm to believe my brother, but reading cues is something I like to think I'm good at.

"Bloody hell. Heads out of the gutter." Yarran sounds entirely pleased with himself. "A *beer*, Patrick." Surprising me, he glances my way and winks.

Is he pushing us together? Reassuring me? I study him a beat, my smile warm as I figure—hell, choose to believe—that's exactly what he's doing.

"What do you want to do, Trev? Baling or...?" I ask, taking control of the conversation since Patrick still hasn't spoken. I'm pretty sure there's a silent discussion going on between him and his friend, but it's no longer something I'm worried about.

"I'm good on the tractor. I've been on it before at least. I just need to know how the baler works."

"And that means I'll be wherever you need me to be." I keep my voice light, not taking on the gruffer tones my head is encouraging me to use when I imagine various options.

"Yeah, thanks. We can figure that out in the morning." Patrick's found his voice, but his blush hasn't quite calmed. I'm not used to seeing him flustered. Not going to lie, I like seeing him floundering a little. It makes me feel less out of my depth.

"Sounds good. One more for the road?" Yarran's already standing as we all bob our heads.

———

The morning's been perfect. Not too hot at a glorious twenty-seven degrees Celsius, just the right amount of breeze to keep us cool, and some refreshing clusters of clouds to shield us from the sun a few times an hour.

Patrick and I are sitting on the tailgate of the side by side. He's just finished fixing the water pump with my awesome assistance of passing him tools, and we're taking a ten-minute breather before we start poisoning some fence lines. Peering at him, I ask, "Do you miss it?"

He angles my way, a couple of creases settling on his brow. "What's that?"

"This." I give a chin lift in the general direction before me. "Living out here, having so much space?"

Placing the lid back on the bottle of water, he shrugs. "When I'm out here and it's all going well, then sure. But times can be tough."

I bob my head. In the time we've known each other, I'm aware the area's been hit by severe flood and, on the flipside of that, some pretty major drought. There's been plenty of it around the state and the country, but some places have definitely been hit harder than others.

"You're grafting all the time, you know?" He stares out into the distance, and I follow his gaze. With so much rain over the past couple of years, most of the pasture's green, the dams are full, and the cattle are healthy. There are just a couple of areas yellowing off with native grasses, a few glimpses of the rich red dirt just about visible. "But the town's great, and there's good people around."

"Would you ever move back?" I stare at his

profile, following the curves of his nose, and my eyes roam his masculine jaw. Not for the first time, I wonder what changed? What finally made me lock at him differently? What is it about Patrick that made me completely reassess everything I thought I knew about myself?

He cracks his neck, a pop of bone making me wince. He catches the reaction and smirks. "You don't like that?"

"Not denying it can't feel sadistically good, but the sound…" I turn up my nose. "All levels of gross."

Patrick snorts, his shoulders shaking in amusement. His gaze searches mine as he sobers. "I don't know about moving back," he finally says, and I'm not sure if he's sad or reluctant or something else. What I do know is whatever emotion is swirling around him, I prefer it when he's laughing and flirting or simply relaxed.

I want to ask more about his dad's property, what his plan is over the coming months. I spent a year studying to be a physio at uni before I changed my mind and went into teaching. That year taught me enough to know there's no chance his dad is going to be mobile enough to keep on top of this place. Parting my lips to speak, I pause. Patrick's expression looks weary, so I leave it alone.

I go to change the subject, but he surprises me by saying, "I suppose this is where I always imagined myself settling down."

I clamp my mouth shut and stare at him wide-eyed.

Angling to look at me, he chuckles. "Don't look so surprised. I dread to know the stories your brother's told you about me." While he's joking, there's a layer of nerves I'm not used to seeing from him.

"Believe it or not, Patrick," I say, aiming for levity, "you're not at the centre of every conversation me and Trev have." I quirk a brow at him.

"Damn, hit me where it hurts, why don't you."

I roll my eyes. "I think your ego will remain intact for another day." I don't want to let go of what he shared though, so I ask, "And settling down, that's something you want?" Curiosity surrounds my words, and maybe a little longing too. It's crazy, right? How the hell can I long for a person I hooked up with once. More specifically, a man who's flirted with me for so long to only turn my head years later, and as far as I know, for no particular reason than me thinking *what-if.*

And honestly, I'm not even sure if that's the truth of it.

One minute we were having a great time in Bali,

with the usual flirting and fun. The next there was a moment of clarity almost, a moment where the veil lifted, and I felt like I really saw him for the first time.

Well, that and my dick liked the idea a fuck of a lot.

"What are you thinking about?"

His question jolts me from my musings. I notice he hasn't answered my question, unless of course he did and I zoned out.

"Hmm?" I play dumb.

"That look on your face. You were thinking hard about something."

With our gazes connected, I struggle to pull away, too many thoughts buzzing through my mind. "Trev calls it my constipated face." I laugh it off, not willing to risk a deeper conversation.

"Your brother can be an arsehole."

"Right." I grin. "Pleased it's not just me."

"And speaking of arseholes, I suppose we better head back. Make sure Trev's doing okay before we start the fence lines."

There's nothing I can do but nod. The unanswered question will have to remain between us. While it's a little frustrating, and I'm particularly frustrated with myself for not knowing how to handle how I'm feeling, I've learned something new about Patrick.

At some point he wants to settle down. The knowledge wraps around me, warm and exciting. It's totally possible I'm getting way ahead of myself, like a lot, but maybe the reason relationships I've had with women never stuck, never felt quite right, like something was missing, was because I was waiting to pull the blinders away and see Patrick in a whole new light.

CHAPTER 10

PATRICK

"D ID YOU HEAR ABOUT THE GUY WHO DIPPED HIS testicles in glitter?"

I don't look up. Can't. Not when my head is close to a pair of nuts and I'm trying to band them up.

Not caring no one's responded, Alec continues, "Yeah, he had pretty nuts."

"Jesus fucking Christ." Trev groans, and I imagine he's shaking his head. He's standing at the gate lever, waiting to release the bull calf once I've finished snapping the band around its sac. "If I have to hear another shitty joke about balls, I'm going to take one of these bands and use it on you."

"Okay, okay, how about this one? What do you call a snowman with no testicles?" Alec barely waits a second. "*Sno* balls."

I snort, more at Trev cussing at his brother rather than Alec's lame jokes. "Okay. Done." I stand upright, my knees cracking.

Trev opens the head bale, and the calf races out. "That was the last bull calf, right?"

I bob my head, relieved. Usually banding is super straightforward, but every now and then, there's a saggy fucker who's a nightmare. "Yeah. Just the last few to spray and vaccinate."

Earlier this morning, we ran the cattle in the yards. Pretty soon after that, we got to work.

Trev took care of getting their heads in the head bale and added tags to the newest calves, while I focussed on banding, spraying, and pushing them through the crush, and Alec became a whizz with the 7-in-1 vaccine.

The sun's high in the sky and I'm starving by the time we finish. Having the guys here has helped massively. The last hour and a half especially they found their stride and were at it like pros. It's made for a long morning, though.

"Let's head back and grab some lunch. Then we'll round up the next lot."

"No rest for the wicked, huh?" Alec's at my side with a smile. Once again, his face is smeared with dirt and dust. He also has a fair amount of cow shit on him, too, like we all do. Fortunately, not on his face.

"You enjoying yourself?"

There's the usual brightness in his eyes that I love seeing, but sun-kissed and wearing one of my old Akubras again, he looks especially happy.

"I really am. Got a bit of a buzz by it all, truth be told." He flashes me an adorable smile.

We settle into the side by side, Alec next to me and Trev on the seat behind me. Flooring it, we race to the main house, Alec grinning widely at my side as the breeze whips at him. Holding down his hat, he chuckles when we hit a small bump, all of us jolting. Hearing his laugh, I don't slow down, despite Trev grumbling behind me.

With smudges on his face and laughing loudly, Alec seriously fits here. I've never seen him look quite so at ease, so full of carefree joy, and that's saying something since the guy is super relaxed and positive.

When I pull up, Alec lets out a whoop, and I chuckle as he gets out. Our gazes connect, and not for the first time today, my breath catches. He's so incredibly handsome.

"These things are such good fun." He pats the Can-Am. "I never realised they could go so fast."

"Right. Can hit 70 kph. Not that I would out here with all the uneven ground."

"Even at twenty, they're fun."

Brightness shines in his eyes, and I find it hard to pull away. But I do, if only because I'm more than aware Trev is next to us. "Right. Let's wash up and we'll grab lunch. I'll make sure Dad's okay too."

Alec looks down at himself. His nose scrunches. "It's a good job I'm fully grown. What, with all this manure on me…"

Damn straight you're fully grown. As if his words were an open invite, I trail my gaze over him, down his long limbs and back up again, perusing his wide chest. The memory of him naked, all of his delicious skin on display, pushes to the forefront of my brain.

What I wouldn't give to see him that way again. Hell, him naked and wearing my Akubra… now there's a cowboy fantasy I've never had before.

"Yeah, yeah, you're a big boy. We get it." Trev rolls his eyes and nudges Alec. "You stink of shit, so go wash up." He dashes away, laughing as Alec whips a muscular arm out to shove him.

"Piss off," Alec hollers after Trev, nothing but humour in his tone. With his brother gone, he peers at me. "You washing up first in the cabin or…?"

I swear the way he's looking at me isn't so

dissimilar to that night in Bali. Interest, want, curiosity. But I'm so fucking terrified I can't read him properly that I clear my throat and shake my head, saying, "I'll wash up in the main house."

Still smiling, Alec bobs his head. "No worries. More hot water for me." He winks, then heads towards the cabin.

Of course I watch him stroll away. His arse in those jeans is the very definition of sinful. Full and pert like a mouth-watering peach. In December, I spent no time worshipping his backside, but oh how I want to.

With a shake of my head, trying to dislodge the visual of Alec's perfect arse, I make my way to the house. Alec and I are heading out west on Thursday. A night under the literal stars, just the two of us. My dick twinges, ignoring my attempts to not get excited about being truly alone with Alec.

It makes sense to take lube, right, and a condom, you know, just in case? Better to be prepared. I hold on to that thought, let my imagination take flight. How can it not, since Alec's been sweet and friendly and I'm absolutely sure flirty since being here?

Smiling at the possibility, I step into the house, calling, "Dad? Where are you?"

"Out the back."

After kicking off my boots, I follow the sound of his voice. My smile slips. Outside on one of the chairs, his leg perched on a large footstool, Dad's red and sweaty. "What's going on?"

His gaze shifts to me. Guilt and defiance sparkle in his eyes.

"Dad, seriously, what have you done?"

"Nothing. I'm fine. I've just finished my damn flexes and extensions is all."

I don't sit down opposite him since I'm grubby from my morning with the cattle. Instead, I crouch before him, eyeing him carefully. "You do the required amount?"

The hesitation is clear as day as he purses his lips and glances away.

"Dad." His name's a sigh. "I know you're frustrated and want to race ahead and heal, but if you don't follow your physio's instructions to a T, you're going to do yourself damage. You know this."

A huff of exasperated breath escapes him. "I get it. I was having a good morning is all. Thought I could handle an extra set of exercises." He winces as he shifts slightly, and I know he's in pain.

Being out of action must be a nightmare for him, but he keeps doing stupid shit. It takes a lot to piss me off, but Dad being so dense is pushing my buttons. I grind my teeth together, hating he's in pain, hating he's upset. The longer I'm here and see the reality of his slow healing, the more I worry about how the hell he's going to run the property.

I've got about four weeks or so left here, but what about after?

I take a calming breath and stand, saying, "I know you hate being babied, but I need you to take some pain meds."

"I hate how foggy they make my brain."

"I get that, but you being in pain isn't great either. You're tense as hell." The muscles in his shoulders are so taut, they're impossible to ignore. "It'll slow your healing down," I say pointedly.

We're in the middle of a stare down when Alec appears. He opens the screen door and joins us on the back veranda.

"All okay out here?" He stops at my side, the scent of shower gel mixing just so with his body spray. He smells clean and fresh and so perfectly Alec. I can't help but inhale, allowing myself to relax in his presence.

"Yeah. Just figuring out lunch so my old man can take some painkillers, then go for a sleep when we head back outside this afternoon."

"Sounds like an excellent plan." Alec's jovial

tone, his natural ability to ease tension out of a space, works its magic. "How about after you've slept, we head out to the yards, and you can check that we've done a good enough job?" He's looking directly at Dad. "We can drive on down, you can stretch your legs for a few steps." He bobs his head like it's a done deal. "You getting some meds in now and resting will give you the energy you need."

"That sounds good to me."

I whip my attention to Dad. A large smile splits his face, and he's nodding and peering up at Alec like he's the next coming or something. I don't even have it in me to narrow my eyes or call him out. Not when he's agreed to take his painkillers and get some rest.

"Right." Alec claps his hands, and his body shifts, drawing my attention back to him.

Those gorgeous brown eyes of his slowly peruse up and down my body, and if I wasn't covered in shit, I'd think he liked what he saw a hell of a lot. There's heat there for sure, even when our gazes connect. A cocky grin then slides on his lips, and he quirks a brow at me.

"How about I rustle up some grub while you go and hose down?" The glimmer of heat in his gaze returns, and I like a hell of a lot the idea of Alec thinking about me naked. "Stinking like cow shit isn't the ideal accompaniment to go with sandwiches." He finishes with a full-blown laugh.

When Dad joins in, I roll my eyes and shake my head at them. "Tell me why I thought it was a good idea to have you here when it seems like together you like ganging up on me?"

"Because I have the best ideas." Alec bounces his brows, and fuck if he's not right. I'm so unbelievably grateful he's here. He also works some serious magic with Dad. I think it's the whole teacher thing. He has the ability to get my old man onside with little fuss. Something he's done since the first night of being here.

"That you do." My brain goes to that night in Bali. The dip of my voice has his eyes flaring. I flash him a grin, unable to keep holding back or pussy footing around how I feel about him. Or how much I still want him.

"Jesus." Dad's voice tears my focus away from eye fucking Alec. "I wanted a ham and cheese sandwich with a side of potato chips, not front-row seats to a damn mating ritual."

Heat floods my cheeks, and I splutter unintelligible words. Seriously, what can I say to that beyond flat-out denial, which would be total bullcrap?

Alec's chuckle snaps my attention to him. Bright-eyed and apparently super amused, he bounces his brows at me before turning to Dad. "What, you didn't order some entertainment with your lunch? I'll be back in a jiffy."

When Alec backs away, leaving me and Dad alone, I make to leave and get washed up. Dad pointedly clearing his throat stops me in my tracks.

Making eye contact, he stares me down, holding me in place.

"Out with it." I follow up with an embarrassed huff of breath.

"You've never brought a man home before."

Wide-eyed, I splutter again and shake my head. Apparently he has no clue about the couple of nights Yarran's spent with me in the cottage. "That's not what—"

"Maybe not, but there's clearly something." He bobs his head, and I know his brain is working overtime. I should have given him his pills and ushered him straight to bed. It would have saved me from this moment and wanting the ground to open. It's impossible to not feel like a teenager under Dad's scrutiny.

While he's right, or at least there *was* something back in Bali, I'm not a guy who can easily pour his heart out to anyone. Well, maybe one day, if... I swallow hard and push the desire for more with Alec away. What I feel for him is so far removed from a sexy crush, it's ridiculous.

"I like him. Alec," Dad says.

I nod, not wanting to be a complete arsehole. "Yeah."

"I think him sticking around wouldn't be a hardship. Sounds like he did a good job with the cattle. Plus he's handy to have around."

A chuckle slips free. "So you want me to keep him because he knows some physio techniques and can massage like a champ?"

A shit-eating grin is directed my way. "Yep. Plus he knows how to make a decent runny fried egg. He's a good-looking bloke, too, right?"

"Dad! Jesus."

"And this sounds like the perfect time to interrupt."

My head swivels in the direction of the opening flyscreen door. Broad-shouldered and delectable, Alec's filling the doorway with a cat-that-got-the-cream smirk. "Uhm…" I have nothing.

"I just wanted to check what you'd like to drink." Blazing eyes are directed my way. Amusement dances in their depths, but I know what heat and want looks like on Alec. The memory is etched into my very being. "It sounds like you might be super thirsty." His lips twitch. The move is enough to drag the tension from me and I snort. "Need something long and cool?" The arsehole bounces his brows.

"It's like the second act of a show. Maybe we should have some popcorn too."

There's no need to look at Dad to figure he's grinning and loving my embarrassment.

I roll my eyes and shake my head. "And that's my cue to haul arse and get in the shower."

Heat once again sparks in Alec's gaze, and with the way he does a slow dip down of my body, it doesn't take a genius to work out what he's imagining. I leg it, needing to get away before I pop a boner in front of my dad. No way would he ever let me live it down.

Once in the shower, I relax under the spray. My grin is quick to form. Dad likes Alec. It's not surprising, as he's such an incredible, smart guy. That he's hot as fuck and can drink my cum like he's been doing it for years is simply an added bonus.

Thursday. Just two days until we get some time alone. That gives me time to get over my aversion of putting myself out there and opening up. Because as fun as flirting and dancing around this chemistry is, I want to know if there's a real future possible for the two of us.

It doesn't matter that I have no idea how that will work out or what it'll look like. If we want this badly enough, we'll make it happen.

CHAPTER 11

ALEC

Filled with easy conversation about everything and nothing, the drive was fun. I was a little disappointed when we arrived at Charleville, which meant we were no longer alone. All disappointment fled as quickly as it appeared as we wandered around the observatory, though.

The sky lay before us, crystal clear through the lens, the shivering stars so bright, feeling so near we could touch them.

After a hot chocolate in the cute café, we then headed out to a spot that apparently only locals know about. Once our swags were rolled out, I lit a few mosquito coils, which Patrick chuckled at, then we lay side by side, faces pointed up.

I'm not sure how long we've been lying like this.

What I am sure about is how comfortable I am. There's a buzz in my stomach. It's been there since the day I arrived, but over the last couple of days especially, it's become more persistent, like waves of electricity zipping between connected wires. This feeling has everything to do with the man at my side who's pointing out the few stars he knows.

"It's breathtaking." My voice is a low murmur.

"You do know you're whispering, right?"

I chuckle. "So are you." I shrug and angle to peer at the side of his face. We switched on the small camp light a little while ago. With the moon barely a sliver, it's pitch-black out. While that's awesome to stargaze, it makes seeing my hand in front of my face tricky.

The soft yellow light spills across Patrick's cheek. While I can't make it out, I know there's a little scruff covering it. I'm tempted to reach out and drag my fingers across, missing the whisper of fine hair across my skin. It doesn't matter I've only experienced it once; the memory refuses to fade.

It's warm out. We're both in trackie bottoms, though—an attempt to keep the mozzies from attacking our legs. Our arms are exposed as we're wearing T-shirts. Only a little light reaches the skin on his forearms. It's enough for me to admire the sinewy muscles wrapped in what I know is sun-kissed skin.

"You're so beautiful."

My words turn to static between us and swiftly grab his attention. Patrick's gaze is on me. His eyes are wide. If we had more light, I imagine I'd see blown pupils and maybe a hint of glistening. But here under the blazing stars and the warm lantern light, all I hear is the catch of his breath and the slow exhale that follows.

"You say that to all the guys who take you to see the stars?" While he's still only whispering, there's a tremble there, a tease of emotion that I absolutely feel.

I could hold back, knowing my experience with dating hasn't prepared me for any of this. Prepared me for Patrick. But I don't want to keep my feelings locked down. Instead, I latch onto my emotions of the last few days. My what-if thoughts since last December.

For one experience to have such a hold on me has to mean something.

"Can honestly say you're the only person I've ever said those words to before." With our gazes still connected, I offer the briefest of smiles. Women have been pretty and sexy, but none have compared to the man at my side.

He shifts, leaning on his elbow to peer at me.

More of his face is captured in the gentle light so I can read the emotions jumping across his features.

"You don't believe me." I mirror his position and bob my head. "I get it. Sounds like I'm blowing smoke up your arse."

"And are you?" The carefully controlled tone he's using sounds close to snapping.

"No." I want him to see the truth in my gaze but am happy to give him words if he needs them. "My dating history isn't exactly anything to write home about." It's the truth. I can hook up like a trooper, but something serious? The connection's never been quite right.

"Maybe because you've never told anyone they're beautiful before." There's a softness to his voice that wasn't there a moment ago.

A flutter and a flip and my heart beats so quickly I'm sure if I look down, it's going to be pulsing like a cartoon character's. "I think you're probably on to something." I nod, surprised I can't see sparks zipping between us.

Patrick leans close, his focus dropping to my mouth before darting back to my eyes. His approach is slow, cautious. And I get it. I really do. It's sweet but unnecessary. Not that I'm going to launch at him.

Patrick taking control makes my pulse race. Not

being in the driver's seat all the time is heady and refreshing. It doesn't stop me from angling towards him a little. He needs to know I want this, and I'm not sure I can get my words out without sounding as desperate as I feel.

The pause when his lips are a hairsbreadth from mine is almost my undoing. I stay steady, release a shaky exhale, and finally, fucking finally, his mouth presses to mine.

I can't hold back.

Don't.

Won't.

Couldn't even if my life depended on it.

I tilt my head to the right, drinking in his kiss, parting my lips when his tongue seeks entry. A groan tears out of me at the first touch of our exploring tongues. And then we're moving.

I palm his cheek while he holds the back of my head, his fingers threading through my hair. We kiss until I'm breathless, make out until my head's fuzzy with so much heat lapping at my skin, it's likely we'll set fire to the dry grass around us.

Pushing against me, Patrick eases me back onto my swag. With our mouths still connected, I fall back with a moan, his weight on my chest welcome.

Realising he's slowing down, I wrap my arms

around him, desperate to continue. I could kiss Patrick forever. It's soft and perfect, filled with promises and desire. The way his unshaven face scratches lightly on my chin sends sparks of awareness through me. They land somewhere deep in my chest, transforming to a rightness I can't get my lust-fuelled brain to navigate.

But he's still pulling away.

I groan, making my unhappiness known when I lose his mouth.

His light chuckle stops me from outright complaining, though. He angles up so I can see his expression without going cross-eyed.

"This okay?" Again with the whisper-soft words. They're going to be my undoing.

"You stopping? Hell no." I reach down to grab his waist, manhandling him so he's fully on top of me. I release a contented sigh at the position, choosing to ignore his louder laugh. "Much better, but back to not happy about you stopping."

Despite my confident tone and me pushing myself to ask for what I want, there's no disguising the tremor in my hands. Last time was incredible. If this is another one and done, I'm not sure I'll be able to take that on the chin like last time.

Navigating the intricacies of dating is hard as

fuck. It's why I never do it. A hook-up with a random is nowhere near the same level of pressure.

Patrick is far from an unknown, though.

"What are you thinking?" He tilts his head. There's enough yellow glow for me to see the concern shining in his gaze. Not that it isn't obvious in his tone.

That backbone of mine that threatens to turn to jelly holds strong. "Just hoping I don't fuck this up or that you don't change your mind as soon as we're done with whatever this is."

I applaud myself for communicating while internally rolling my eyes for making this all harder than it needs to be. Last time stung something fierce. These past few days of laughing, working side by side, sharing heated glances combined with the electric kiss we just shared is enough to make me wait him out.

For my own sanity, I need to know where his mind's at.

At my words, he pulls himself to sitting. Maybe I should have kept my big mouth shut. When he doesn't turn away, I take a breath and push myself up, mirroring his position once again.

"I don't think you need to worry about fucking this up."

"No?"

He shakes his head.

Needing to know about the rest of my sentence, I ask, "And how about you changing your mind?"

Watching me closely, Patrick squints as if studying me harder. "Why do you think that's on the cards, me changing my mind?"

I twist my lips, gnawing on them a little. Jesus, I school kids on the merits of honesty, sharing feelings, living their truth. But me getting deep and real? It's ridiculously out of my norm.

Gathering my thoughts, I exhale and angle my head back, taking in the stars. I *will* answer. I want to, but my thoughts are wild. Staring at the vastness overhead reminds me I'm one soul amongst the billions on this planet. Any words I share now will get caught in the gentle autumn breeze, carrying them away. But not until Patrick hears them first.

I want that.

With renewed determination, I peer at Patrick. He's waiting patiently for me. His gaze steady, his breaths even.

"This is a lot," I admit. "Maybe too much for you."

"Too much?"

"Well, last time, you couldn't get out of my room fast enough." My skin heats at the memory, mortified that I'm saying this to him. But I can't keep dancing around this.

There's a beat of silence. He's studying me, gaze tracing my expression, seeming to stare so hard he's trying to peer into my soul. "You mentioned a bucket list."

"Huh?" My face scrunches in confusion. I have no idea what he's talking about.

"A bucket list," he repeats. He hesitates and tugs his lip beneath his top teeth, gnawing there for a moment. "After, you said something about you could tick off something in your bucket list." I can tell he's embarrassed, probably as mortified as I am confused. "I just thought that was it, you know. Something ticked off your list and you were done." Discomfort morphs his features, probably because I'm staring at him like he's got two heads.

I part my lips, once, twice, three times before I can start speaking. "I have no clue what you're talking about." Shaking my head, I continue to stare at him, hoping it'll jog my memory or at least help me figure this out. When he frowns, I shake my head again, completely baffled. "Bucket list? What bucket list?" I don't give him time to answer, saying, "I don't have a bucket list."

"You… you don't?"

"No. Well, you know I have a couple of places overseas I'd like to visit one day, but not a bucket list. Jesus, I don't even write a shopping list."

The rise and fall of Patrick's chest is exaggerated as he seems to be steadying his breathing. "So I wasn't—"

"Hell no," I say quickly, not bearing to hear whatever he has to say. "Bali was incredible. You opened my eyes to a part of me I never knew existed. Hands down best sex of my life." With the sound of my heart pounding in my ears, I give myself a moment to calm. That I've just admitted that to him is embarrassing, but clearly we've confused the hell out of each other. Misread each other, frustratingly so.

"Because that's what it was. Amazing. When you left, I was gutted," I admit. Emotion rushes to my chest, hot with discomfort. "Figured… I don't know, that you weren't interested in more."

"God, no. I am so interested in more." The muscles in his jaw flex when he closes his mouth. "It was my best night, too, with you. I can't believe I bolted. What a fucking idiot." He's pissed with himself, and I can totally relate. I'm pissed off at myself too.

Patrick leans in my direction again, considering me carefully. His expression shifts to one I can't quite read, but he does tilt his head slightly, and I'm pretty sure he's looking at me fondly. Which is great and all, but I'd much prefer the heat of a few minutes ago.

Making out. Counting stars. Blowing our loads. Things I could all safely indulge in now if Patrick really means what he's been saying.

"Ask me the question again."

Patrick's words are so quiet, I pull my hand away, needing to pay attention. "What question?"

"About me changing my mind." A new gruffness has entered his tone. It grabs my awareness and holds tight.

"Will you?"

I haven't finished speaking before he's already shaking his head. The movement shoots awareness across my skin. Goosebumps chase along after, and I'm hyperaware of the crackling energy buzzing in the small distance between us.

"In Bali, running was the worst decision I've ever made," he clarifies. "I should have just talked it out with you. I knew it was your first time with a guy." He winces. "It was really shitty of me to leave you like that."

Surprise rattles me. "Oh, uhm... I didn't think about it like that. I just thought you weren't interested in a repeat. Maybe heard I was a snuggler," I add with a low laugh. It earns me a small smile. The next is a little harder to admit. Heat crawls up my neck as I say, "I thought maybe you'd got me out of your system or something. After so many years of flirting and foreplay, I was an itch you finally scratched." A light shrug that's clearly so far from casual lifts my shoulders. "And that would be fine," I quickly add. "No shame in one-night stands."

"Fuck no." The intensity of Patrick's words startles me. His hand lands on mine, both balancing on my knee. "That's so way off base."

"It is?" Hope unfurls in my chest, pure and wonderful.

"That night you cemented yourself in even deeper... It was amazing. Beyond anything I've ever imagined. And honestly, Alec, I've thought about a night with you a lot." A shy smile graces his lips, and fuck if I can stay away.

I lean forwards and capture his mouth.

There have been enough words for now. I've heard all that I need, and unless I'm still being dense, I figure that we both want the same thing.

Tonight, and I'm pretty confident a tomorrow, too.

CHAPTER 12

PATRICK

Exhaustion beats at me. But wrapped around Alec, my head on his chest and his fingers playing with my hair, still being wide awake as we watch the sunrise is totally worth it. We haven't slept at all. All night we've alternated between hot-as-hell kisses, mind-blowing frotting, talking about our jobs, our families, our everyday lives, and everything in between.

There was a mutual handjob in there too.

And each second has been perfect.

Pink and orange streak across the horizon, and the few stars that remain visible begin to fade. Our voices are low. No longer quite a whisper, but quiet enough to not startle the increasing number of kookaburras laughing their wake-up call.

Alec pauses playing with my hair for a jaw-cracking yawn. I angle to watch him wipe at his face before his gaze snaps to mine, a sweet smile curving his lips.

"You doing okay there?"

He chuckles. "Yeah. Not used to pulling all-nighters."

With a groan, I stretch, moving away so I don't sock Alec in the face. Bones pop and creak. We've snuggled together in my swag all night, and while there's padding, there's no mistaking we're on the hard ground. "Not sure my body is a fan either." I follow up with my own yawn. "Thank Christ we don't have a busy day."

"Even if we have, I have no regrets."

The softness of his words is a gentle caress. They pull a smile from me and definitely deserve a kiss. "Totally worth it," I agree, leaning over to press my lips against his. It's just a quick peck that could easily turn into more, but the thought of coffee is calling my name.

When I ease away, he grumbles, "That all I'm getting?"

"Kisses or coffee? Your call."

Indecision morphs his features. "Can't I have both?"

I snort and slant my mouth over his, sighing into Alec's touch, his taste. When his tongue flicks against mine, blood rushes south, my cock chubbing. He's so good at this. Kissing. Making me lose my mind until he becomes the centre of everything.

With a swift tug, Alec hauls me closer. I go willingly, landing on top of him. Our boxer-covered dicks touch, and I kiss him deeper, taking control as I rut against him. He parts his legs further, wrapping one around me. Its perfect weight against my arse encourages me to move faster.

When he jerks his hips, seeking more contact, I tear my mouth from his with a deep groan. "Jesus." I don't stop rutting as I peer down at him. "You're so hot."

He jerks against me again, and I fight not to close my eyes. At half mast, his expression is heated. Squeezing my arse cheek, he watches me carefully. A delicious shudder rips through me, earning me a satisfied smile. Earlier, when he wrapped his palm around my cock, he knew exactly how to work my dick and had me coming in an embarrassingly short amount of time. His hand on my arse, though, the thought of his thick fingers exploring… Jesus, just the idea of it has me needing more.

"I want you to come in my mouth again."

Alec's words have me locking up. Desire ripples across my skin, and the visual threatens to unravel me. "You can have anything you want."

The smile he sends me stretches. "In that case, let's switch."

Not having to be told twice, I scramble off him, flip onto my back, and tear off my boxers. By the time I'm done, I'm a panting, needy mess of impatience, and Alec's chuckling and staring down at me with open amusement.

"Like that idea, huh?"

I bob my head. "So fucking much." I clamp onto my dick as it swells, the promise of his hot mouth driving my need to new heights.

"You're not worried I'll mess this up and not get you off?" While Alec's still looking entertained by my eagerness, the edge of uncertainty is loud and clear.

I sit up and reach for him. He comes willingly, sitting on my lap. Ignoring my throbbing dick that's totally on board with this position, I rub a soothing hand over his back. "Everything you want to do to me, I'll love. I swear you could blow a hot breath on my dick, and I'd come, because it's you who's paying me attention."

There's a slight shift in his muscles as tension slips away. "I feel the same way."

"Yeah?"

"Definitely. I like you a fuck of a lot." Pink crawls up his neck, settling high on his cheeks.

A happy grin curves my lips. "I like you a fuck of a lot too." That he's putting himself out there is a major turn on. "Whatever we do will be amazing, and if you change your mind or want to stop, that's okay too. It always will be, okay?"

Tracing his fingers across my collarbone, he bobs his head. "So…" Emotion shifts in his eyes as he drags that word out, and I grin in preparation, knowing he's calmer and what we've discussed seems to have hit the mark. "The baby-queer pep talk is over, right? I can get to sucking you off?"

He startles a laugh from me. "Feel free to lick and suck me like a Zooper Dooper."

A huff of a chuckle escapes him. It's quickly wiped away when he captures my mouth in a searing kiss. I hang on, letting him take everything he wants and needs. By the time he works his kisses down my neck and urges me to fall back, small vibrations ripple along my skin.

Alec doesn't hover. Doesn't hesitate. There's no attention to my nipples or stomach or the expanse of skin between my neck and my groin. Like a heat-seeking missile, his mouth is on my cock, sucking my head like it really is a Zooper Dooper and he's desperate for the icy pole to keep him cool on a scorching day.

"Holy fucking hell." The words are torn out of me when he swallows deeper.

A low vibration from his throat has me clenching and gasping, and while the sun has risen, I see stars. I tilt my head back, lost to sensation. Lost to the wet coating my cock, the red-hot suction. Fuck. I'm lost to him. To Alec.

He's everything I dreamed of and more.

A tight grip appears at the root of my cock, and I snap my gaze down, needing to see Alec. With his eyes closed, he looks debauched, perfect, and like he's enjoying each slide of his tongue on the underside of my dick.

"That's it, baby." There's reverence in my praise. How can there not be when he's taking me in like a champ and seems to love every moment?

When he blinks his eyes open, our gazes connect and hold. I'm frozen, caught completely in the power I know this man has over me.

With an unwavering gaze, he slows, and I bite my lip. His focus darts to my mouth before shifting again to make eye contact. Then slowly, so fucking slowly I begin to unravel, he presses forwards, swallowing my cock until he gags. My dick throbs, turning to steel when he doesn't pull away. Instead, he eases down further until I'm in his throat.

He holds in position, his nostrils flaring. Saliva drips to my balls, and I'm gone.

"Fuck, fuck, fuck." As warnings go, it's pretty explicit, but not soon enough to have him pulling away. I shoot my load, my arms giving way as I release.

He shifts back, choking, pulling off to inhale.

It's on the tip of my tongue to apologise, but I can't form words. My cum's still spilling out of my dick, and it's taking everything in me to stay consci—

"Holy fucking… nnngh." My shoulders jerk, my words flying free when Alec latches back on, sucking and drinking me down.

I have to see.

Jesus. He looks blissed out. At the sight, my cock gives once last pulse, a fresh spurt falling free. And Alec's still there, groaning, head slowing to a gentle bob. His eyelids flutter open as he pulls away. His gaze remains on my dick, though, and I want to speak, want to praise, but the small smile that appears on his face has me catching my breath. Leaning down, he places the gentlest of kisses to my spent cock before his eyes dart to mine.

Unable to speak through the emotion clawing at my throat at seeing so much reverence, so much beauty, I sit up and haul him towards me. Tingles still wrack my body, but I need to kiss him, show him how incredible he is.

The kiss is slow, tender. Tasting myself is always kind of hot, but mixed with Alec's sweet kisses, it's delicious. The only thing that would make this better is the addition of Alec's cum.

Trailing my mouth across his cheek and to his neck, I say, "Ease back. I want to—"

The shake of his head cuts me off.

"No?"

Alec's flushed cheeks turn bright red. "I already came."

Satisfaction unfurls deep in my chest. "Yeah?"

Burying his face against my neck, he huffs in quiet amusement. "Oh yeah. Thought I was going to black out there for a minute."

With a smile, I dot a kiss to the top of his head. That he came from sucking me off has me practically puffing out my chest with pride. "Did you touch yourself?" I'm totally putting him under the spotlight, but apparently I'm needy as hell.

"Just got some friction going on your swag." Hearing the smile in his words, I encourage him to ease back and look at me. His gaze turns shifty. "Your swag is going to need to soak for a while."

I laugh loudly and spread kisses across his jaw. "It was already wrecked from our handies. Totally worth it."

He bobs his head and makes eye contact. I see the question there that I've yet to answer.

"You were amazing," I say in earnest, shaking my head in wonder. "You deep throated me. How the fuck did you do that? I thought I was going to pass out with how good it felt. Not going to lie, you may have sucked a few of my brain cells out." Punctuating my words by squeezing his arse, I stare up at him, enjoying the satisfaction entering his gaze.

"Totally worth the practice."

I freeze at his words. Practice? Fuck, has he spent the last few months developing his deep-throating skills? Knowing I have no right to be pissed or hurt, I keep my mouth shut and nod. There's no chance my words or tone wouldn't give away the jealousy weaving into my thoughts.

"What is it? You just tensed." His brow furrows. "Shit, am I too heavy?" He makes to move, but I stop him with another squeeze to his backside.

"You're perfect to stay right where you are." While he nods, his frown hasn't shifted. I don't want to worry him, which means I'm going to have to either get over myself or tell him my thoughts. Probably both. "Since December, have you been exploring being bi… queer?" Since he hasn't landed on a label, not that he has to, I hedge my bets.

"Yeah." He dances his fingers through the hair on my chest. His lips quirk, and rather than focusing on the green trying to claw its way into my thoughts, I smile back. Alec being confident, exploring, discovering more about his sexuality is amazing. *It's a good thing*, I remind myself.

"Ross and Dan took me to Bar QK for a night out. It was fun."

I lock the jealousy down further, shoving it in a steel cage, and slamming the door shut. "Yeah, I know the place. The drag shows are a riot. Did it help?"

"It was good being around so many people being open. Holding hands, some making out, so many same-sex couples. While I have Ross in my life, I didn't realise how… I don't know, how hetero my world was. It was enlightening."

"That's great." And I mean it. "And the practicing?" As soon as the words leave my mouth, I want to claw them back. I really don't want to know, but I can't *not* ask.

"I've never been a fan of online shopping until I received a whole range of rubber cocks through the post." He chuckles as he speaks, and it takes a beat for his words to register.

My brows shoot high. "That's how you've been practicing? With toys?" My tone is gentle.

He nods, another flush appearing. "Yeah, that and a shitload of porn. I even paid for the good stuff."

Fuck. A relieved laugh shoots from deep within my chest. "That's fucking amazing."

Wide-eyed and looking bemused, Alec stares at me. "O-kay." He drags out. "It's just porn and dildos. Oh, and a butt Fleshlight." His eyes sparkle. "So fucking awesome." He nods emphatically. "Seriously. Hands down the best purchase I've ever made."

Feeling wired and full of feelings that I absolutely cannot share, I gather him close and tug his face to mine. "I can guarantee when you've had a taste of my arse, you'll never be needing or wanting the Flesh-light again."

With parted lips, Alec's eyes widen. A soft "Oh" escapes before he bobs his head. "That sounds perfect to me. You want to start now?"

I grin against his mouth, stealing a kiss. "How

about we save it for a real bed and when we've got lots of lube?" Deciding to leave my lube at home wasn't the best idea I've ever had.

Disappointment morphs his features, lighting me up from the inside. It's hard to fathom how much he wants me, but I refuse to challenge or question it. Alec's a grown man, one who's been on a journey of self-discovery. That it's led him to me, to us sharing this night together, is not something I'll take for granted.

Nor do I want it to ever end.

Logistics be damned. We'll figure out how to make this work. After years of wanting him, I'm not going to let something as simple as work and distance stand in our way.

CHAPTER 13

ALEC

Nodding to let Patrick know I heard him, I stand taller and glance over the sea of hats in the crowd, waiting to spot the first float in the street parade. There's nothing yet, but a band's started playing. We're standing halfway along the closed-off main street in the centre of Roma, so I don't expect it'll be long before I see something.

"What float's Sienna on again?" I ask.

"Her school one," Graham answers.

He woke up surly, was a grump the whole car ride, but he's finally looking relaxed and has even laughed a time or two since being in town. The borrowed wheelchair remains a bone of contention. I'm with Patrick on this one, though. With so many people around, and us standing shoulder to shoulder along the street, it would be too risky for him not to be in a wheelchair.

"Look out for maroon. It's their school colour," he clarifies.

"Got it." I grip the handles of the wheelchair, relieved I've got something to hold on to. With Patrick slightly behind me, his shoulder pressed against my back, not reaching out to hold his hand is a struggle.

In truth, it's so busy that no one would notice, but that isn't the issue at all. Holding hands is the gateway to neck kisses and popping boners. Yeah, nah, getting an erection in the middle of an Easter parade is not my idea of a good time.

Though, he does smell incredible. It doesn't matter that I probably smell the same, courtesy of us sharing a shower this morning and me using his deodorant. Patrick's draw is his own fresh, woodsy scent beneath those fragrances.

Even now my mouth waters at the thought of trailing my tongue down—

"What's got you thinking so hard and catching your breath like that?"

Fucking hell. I release a shuddery exhale. He spoke the words so close to my ear, he may as well have been sucking my lobe. I clear my throat. "No idea what you're talking about. Just waiting for the parade that's drawn all these folks to town."

"Uh-huh."

Jesus. Weak knees are a legit consequence of Patrick darting a light kiss to the skin below my ear.

"Have we decided on the motocross, the mud buggies, or the Four X races?" Trevor's been fixed on his phone for a while now, trying to get some semblance of a plan together. I'm grateful that he's in organisation mode if it means he hasn't seen me get flustered. "Shit, or the drag races. I forgot about those. We're definitely watching the speedway, though, right?"

"Yeah. I think we all said yes to the speedway. I'm easy about the rest." Patrick peers over at Graham. "What do you want to do, Dad?"

"I've done it all before, son. I don't mind."

Patrick bobs his head. "Up to you guys, then," he says to me and Trevor. "Neither of you have done Easter in the Country before, so your call."

Trevor peers over at me. "There's drag racing in the morning, too, so perhaps we cross that off our list."

"Sounds good," I agree. "How about the horses? We can have a little flutter?"

My brother grins. "Sounds good."

The sound of cheers drags all our attention back to the street. The first truck pulling a float is close. There's a bunch of kids dancing on it, wearing… I squint to try to figure out what I'm seeing. "Are they dressed up as *Star Wars* characters?"

At my side, Patrick chuckles. "Looks that way."

"Huh. So not necessarily Easter-themed?"

"Hell no. It's pretty much a free-for-all."

A few people walk along the side with buckets, collecting coin donations. The float holds a variety of signage indicating a charity they're affiliated with and where they're from. This one's a local dance studio.

The kids dancing in *Star Wars* costumes are also throwing out wrapper-covered lollies and mini chocolate eggs. They're clearly having fun, and it's easy to get caught up in the entertainment and good moods surrounding me.

By the time Sienna's school float arrives, my hands are stinging from clapping. My grin's genuine, though. When she spots us right along the edge, she waves frantically.

"Are they characters from *The Addams Family*?" At this point I'm not sure why I'm surprised by the weird and wonderful range on display. The kids, clearly ranging from primary to high school, look awesome.

"Yeah." During the last fifteen minutes, Patrick's hand has gravitated to my waist. While the move had taken my breath away, because apparently I've regressed to a teen with a crush, I like it there a lot. The last time I had any success at dating was at uni, which was a heck of a long time ago. None of the hook-ups have been more than that, and the few times friends have fixed me up didn't stick.

So this right here, cosying up to Patrick, feeling like we're a couple, should feel more unnatural. It's so far removed from that, I keep glancing at him to make sure he's real. Well, that and he's fucking delectable. With his cotton-soft check-shirt's sleeves rolled up, putting his tanned arms on display, it's hard not to spend my time trailing my fingers over the defined muscles in his forearms.

And that his shirt's tucked into his Wranglers, held up by a brown leather belt, brings me so close to drooling that I wonder where this country-vibe cowboy fixation I have sparked from. Because hell if I'm not nearly panting over the image he creates.

A visual of Patrick unzipping, tucking his jeans under his dick, and ramming into me while he's fully dressed slams into me. Jesus. This is not the time or the place. I shake off the thoughts, storing them away for when we're apart and I need to jerk off.

"Ness said the school is performing *The Addams Family* musical," Patrick clarifies, jolting me into awareness. It's the reminder I need to lock down my desire.

"Cool." I discreetly clear my throat. "Well, Sienna makes for an awesome zombie bride." She looks seriously adorable.

We watch the parade, smiling about the costumes, throwing coin donations, and managing to swipe a few mini Easter eggs during the hour-long festivities. Once it's finished, there's a mass exodus of people flooding the no longer cordoned-off main street, heading in a variety of directions to one of the ten or so things to do.

"Breakfast?" my brother suggests.

We all agree and head to one of the trailers serving food. It's not long before we're digging into our bacon and egg rolls. We've managed to snag one of the plastic tables too, so are sitting reasonably comfortably.

"You made it."

It takes me a beat to locate the voice, and when I do, I smile at Yarran. He reaches out and shakes our hands, smiling big.

"Great float," Patricks says, referring to the SAC float Yarran was involved in.

"Thanks, mate. The group worked hard on it. Gotta say, I'm pleased it's all over, though. I'll happily not see a staple gun for the next year." He pulls off his hat and rubs a hand through his thick dark hair. "What are you guys up to?"

Trevor reels off our plans, and Yarran agrees to catch up with us tomorrow at the rodeo. We stay put and work on finishing our coffees. Trevor's chatting to Graham about something, so I turn my attention to Patrick.

His seat's pulled close to mine, his arm on the back of my chair.

"Are you having a good time?"

He nods and faces me head-on. A warm smile tilts his lips. The way he stares, with unhidden heat, is close to disarming me. "I really am. Already this is the best Easter I've ever had."

"Yeah?" There's no subtlety in my breathless question.

"Definitely." He surprises me by leaning forwards and dotting a kiss on my lips. It's fast and totally G-rated, but it's enough to have my pulse speeding up. "That okay, for me to do that in public?" Heat coats his cheeks. "Which I absolutely know I should have checked with you first."

"No. I mean yes, you can show me as much PDA as you want," I rush to say. "And no, you didn't need to check."

Happiness swirls between us. I imagine a cheesy movie and soft music playing to add to the romance of the moment. Instead, there are kids laughing and squealing, the scent of bacon in the air, and—

"Is that a camel?" I do a double take. Ambling down the street are two camels. They're kitted out with harnesses and being led.

Patrick's loud laughter catches my attention. "It sure is." Amusement lights up his features, apparently delighted at my confusion.

"Jesus, this place is insane." I shake my head in wonder. Time on Graham's property has been such good fun. Hard work, too, but I've enjoyed it, and not just because I'm getting hot and heavy with Patrick. And the town—especially with this type of event that transforms its usually sleepy nature into a festival—is incredible.

Glancing around, I take it all in. There are tourists around for sure, but you can spot quite a few of the locals too. That's nothing to do with me knowing them, though Graham does seem to know almost everyone, and has had so many short conversations I'm sure his throat is croaky. It's more to do with their ease as they're wandering around. Their easy smiles. Maybe some of the cowboy boots and Akubras too.

"I love it here."

At my declaration, Patrick's warm hand squeezes my shoulder. "It's a good town with good people."

Switching my attention to him again, I think back to earlier conversations about him being young and eager to leave. Teaching has taught me that needing to fly the coop is the norm. In the small-ish town where my school is located, the students feel the same. The difference is, within an hour and a half they can be in the city, and just half an hour takes them to a much bigger town.

Roma suits Patrick, though, whether he believes it or not. While he hemmed and hawed about the possibility of ever returning, I call bullshit. He likes this place more than he lets on.

"Right." Trev claps his hands, grabbing our attention. "Shall we roll?"

"Lead the way," Graham says with a chuckle, and I grin, happy he seems to be having a good time. I know it's been challenging for him being so cooped up.

We spend time drifting around the market stalls

before checking out the classic cars. We have some time to kill before heading to the racetrack.

We're admiring a 1971 Ford Falcon when Ness catches up with us. After a quick conversation and praising Sienna for how brilliantly she did on the float, they head to the art show. Graham goes with them to look at his grandkids' artwork.

"Are you into cars?" I ask Patrick. We've still so much to learn about each other, and I'm having fun peppering him with questions.

He shrugs. "I can admire a muscle car and the sound of a beefy engine, but I'm not hung up on them, you know?"

I nod in agreement. "They're not my thing either. I was too focussed on sports growing up to pay much attention."

"I know about you playing footie and swimming," he says, reaching for my hand as we continue our walk around the cars. "What other sports?"

Trevor pipes in with "Is rollerblading a sport?"

"Piss off. You're just jealous you look like Bambi on acid when wearing skates." I nudge my brother, my lips twitching.

"Rollerblading, huh?" Amusement surrounds Patrick's words.

"You don't get thighs like these just playing footie," I jest.

The heat in Patrick's eyes is sudden and comes without warning. I wonder if he's recalling kneading my thighs this morning while he was sucking me off in the shower.

I clear my throat before my brother calls me out. He's been so patient and takes what's happening between me and his friend in his stride. I don't want him to feel like a third wheel and get pissed off or uncomfortable.

"Alec?"

Startling at the sound of my name, I spin, losing Patrick's hand in the process of searching for the speaker. "Holy shit." I step forwards, clasp James's offered hand, and clap him on the back. A wide, surprised grin stretches my lips as I pull way, taking in the man before me. "The hell are you doing here?" I shake my head, struggling to marry seeing one of my old uni buddies here of all places. "Jesus, I haven't seen you in—"

"Nope. No saying that out loud. It'll flag how long it's been since finishing uni." Bright-eyed and big-smiled, James looks incredible. Seriously, he's hardly changed. "Mate, it's good to see you, and you're here of all places."

"Right, so Roma, you just here for the long week-end?" I ask.

"Nah, mate. I live here now."

"No shit." My brows shoot high. "You're teaching here?"

"Yeah. Over at the private school. Been here six years now."

"Good on ya."

"What about you? Work? Life?"

"Yeah, pretty damn awesome. Living out at the Sunny Coast, in the hinterland there. Been at the same school for a while. Just taken on a new role as deputy head of house."

"That's great. Congrats. So you're here for the weekend?" James flicks his gaze to over my shoulder.

Shit. So thrown about seeing James after all this time, I forgot my manners apparently.

"Yeah," I answer and take a step to the side, turning to include Trevor and Patrick. "I'm here with my brother, Trev." I glance at Trevor, saying, "James and I studied for our teaching degree together. Trev, James. James, Trev."

"Good to meet you, mate," Trevor says, shaking hands.

When James's gaze shifts to Patrick, familiarity flashes in his eyes. "You're Pat, right?" he asks.

Patrick's smile is tight, a little uncertain. "Yeah." He shakes James's hand. "We met?"

"Nah." James shakes his head, looking relaxed. "But you're with Yarran, right?"

The words hit me in the solar plexus and trail down, churning my gut.

"No," Patrick replies quickly. "Yarran's just a friend."

With a chuckle that tenses my body, James says, "Sorry, mate. *Friends*. Got it."

Discomfort slices through me. This is seriously awkward. While I never asked Patrick, nor has he shared with me any details, I'd assumed something had gone on between him and Yarran. When Yarran stopped by, though, he relaxed me enough, practically pushing me and Patrick together, that I've been able to push my awareness of a possible history aside.

The past is where it should stay. Rationally, I know that, but the reminder tastes like shit.

"Actually…" I expel a breath, shaking myself off and reminding myself I'm not a shrinking violet, nor have Patrick or Yarran done anything wrong. Hell, even James isn't in the wrong here. Four years of studying with the man and I know he's a decent guy. I step next to Patrick and hold his hand. "Patrick and I are together."

Patrick squeezes my palm, and I relax, knowing I did the right thing.

"Oh shit." James's brows shoot so high and his cheeks pinken to such a bright colour that I can't help but chuckle a little. "I'm so sorry. I didn't know, obviously. If I did, I wouldn't be coming across as a prick right now." Looking mortified, James's gaze flickers over us.

"No worries."

James studies me a beat, his shoulders sagging when it's clear I'm being genuine.

"Well, now that awkwardness is over"—he rolls his eyes and repositions his baseball cap—"how about I buy you all a beer, catch up for a bit before you jet off?"

A glance at Trevor tells me he's more than okay with a beer. Turning to Patrick, I raise my brow in question.

"I could do with a cold one before we head to the racetrack."

With that settled, we head to The White Bull Tavern, grab a drink, and chat about old times and new. With Patrick's thigh pressed against mine as Trevor talks about some shit they got up to at uni, I relax, enjoying every moment.

It's easy to imagine this, Patrick and me

together, in a local pub, surrounded by friends, could be our everyday life. The possibility of a future and something very real doesn't feel so unattainable. I place my hand on Patrick's knee and smile contently when he repositions and holds my hand.

***

"How perfect would a hot tub be out here." It's late, and everyone's gone to bed, but Patrick and I are sitting on a bench seat on the small porch outside the cottage.

"Well, maybe off to the side with some sort of privacy around it."

I lean into him and smile. "Good plan." A satisfied breath leaves me as I hold his hand, peering out into the dark. It's only the view of the stars that makes it clear we've not been swallowed whole into nothingness.

"It's been a good day." He punctuates his words with a kiss to the side of my head, and I absolutely agree.

"It's been fun. I like the town when there's so much excitement in the air. But I think I like it sleepy a little more."

"Yeah, me too. Makes navigating around town a whole lot easier."

"A town with one set of traffic lights really does get things backed up when it's so busy." It still blows my mind, places like this. They seem so far removed from what I know and where I live.

A soft yawn escapes Patrick, catching my attention.

"Ready for bed?"

"As long as it's not to sleep."

And just like that, I'm alert, my dick twitching and awareness trickling to my nerve endings. Without speaking, I stand, taking Patrick's hand and helping him up. He comes willingly, his chest pressing against mine, his mouth so close there's no real dipping or stretching necessary.

"You got lots of pent-up energy that needs burning?" Softly trailing my fingers over his shoulders, I wait for his answer, keen to know exactly what he's up for.

"I think I'll always find the energy for you."

My smirk is quick to appear. "Good answer." It's so tempting to take his mouth and get lost in his kisses, but I don't want to be blinded by lust. Well, not yet anyway. "So tonight." Jesus, my mouth's dry and nerves are on the precipice of frazzling. But I want him so fucking badly that I'll risk mortification if it means we get to fuck.

"Yeah?"

"I researched a fair bit about prep." Proud as hell my voice doesn't waver, I continue, "If that's something you're interested in."

A hitch of his breath, a flare of his eyes, and Patrick grips my waist, fingers flexing. "Prep for me or you?" His voice is so low it caresses my skin, feeling like a slow drag of his fingers.

"Me…" My breathing turns shallow. "You." Small vibrations make my voice and limbs tremble. "Either, both, I don't fucking care as long as—"

His lips collide with mine. I groan into his mouth, which he captures by kissing me deeper. We're so close, pressed so tightly together that not even a single sheet of paper could be wedged between us. Kissing him back with everything I have, I tug his shirt out of his jeans. The fantasies I had earlier spur me on. While I absolutely want him to take me like that, now I need him naked. Need to feel his warm skin against mine.

Abruptly, Patrick yanks himself away, his voice gravel when he practically growls, "Come on." And then he's tugging me inside, his eagerness enough to stop me from grumbling. He doesn't pause, doesn't slow his strides as we go into his bedroom. I barely have time to close the door before he's on me.

Need has me reacting.

It's a race to see who can get naked first. Buttons pop, jeans are shoved down, and we stumble onto the mattress together, a laugh huffing out of me at the urgency and the fact our jeans are wrapped around our ankles.

Breaking away, Patrick shoots me a wicked grin. Promise floods his features as he angles away and slowly strips his jeans off, then peels mine away.

The atmosphere shifts at the intensity in his gaze, the reverence in which he finally gets me naked. My pulse gallops, heart thundering, breath hissing out of me as I watch every move he makes.

Both blissfully naked, our content sighs split the air when Patrick lies on top of me.

"I want you to fuck me."

The thumping of my heart is loud in my ears at his declaration. "Okay." My dick turns to steel, wanting in him so badly. "Show me how you want me."

The softening gaze, the punch of emotion I see there, makes my heart stutter.

He bobs his head, kisses me breathless, and only pulls away when I'm clawing at his back and rocking against him. "Let's switch."

I'm moving before he's finished, grabbing him in my hold and spinning us around. Patrick's back hits the mattress with a grunt and a loud chuckle. Smiling at the sound, I peer down at him. "Fan of my smooth moves?"

He snorts and gives a small shake of his head. "A fan of your muscles maybe," he teases, his fingers roaming my chest. "I'll be an even bigger fan if you get the lube and condom out of the drawer."

Anticipation, a live wire in my veins, threatens to lock up my muscles and have me shooting my load before I can even move. "Fucking hell." I groan, sitting up and grabbing onto the base of my cock. "If I come when my fingers are in your arse, you're not going to judge, right?" I'm totally serious, as it's a real possibility.

Patrick swallows hard before expelling a slow, shaky breath. "Just the thought of your fingers in my arse is getting me close, so I think we'll be even if that happens."

A rumbling laugh spills out of me, amused and so relieved that Patrick and I are like this. Can talk this sort of shit out. I stretch my neck like I'm doing a warm-up, causing Patrick's lips to twitch and thin as he buries his smile.

I roll my eyes but don't hold back my own smirk.

"If I bust a nut too soon," I say, reaching out and grabbing the lube and condom, "I promise I'll be able to go again."

"You will, huh?" He runs his tongue lightly over his bottom lip as his gaze falls to me opening the lube and slicking my fingers. His nostrils flare, his breathing turning shaky.

In answer, I reach out and press the pad of my finger against his hole. "Open wider for me." He does so immediately, spreading his thighs, and I practically swallow my tongue. Fuck. Like this, Patrick is breath-taking, and that his need is clear to see, flushing his chest and neck, has his dick thickening and all but throbbing, is almost too much.

Never have I been so turned on before. Never have I wanted someone as desperately as I do Patrick.

I rub circles around his opening, my own clenching at the memory of what it felt like when I experimented on myself. When he grips the sheets and pushes down, chasing my fingers, I clamp onto my bottom lip with my teeth and slowly ease in one slick finger.

"Nngh…"

Jesus. That sound. The way his body sucks me in. The bliss battling for dominance in his wild eyes.

"Fuck, you're amazing." I don't stop, don't hesitate pushing all the way in until I'm two joints deep.

"More," he gasps, his hips rocking, dick hard, thick, looking ready to explode.

I push in and out before removing my finger and sliding two inside. "Holy shit." My gaze is fixed on the way he's taking me in. The way he stretches… the way that's going to feel on my dick… I groan, picking up speed, encouraging him to ride my fingers. Tight and hot, his channel is a vice. I blink, trying to clear the static swirling in my mind.

I need inside him before I seriously do come.

"Get in me."

He's as desperate as I am. His moaning's loud, unrestrained. His neck's taut, muscles so tight, I want to bite down and lick a long trail across them, savouring every slick of sweat and inch of skin.

"One more." I'm panting now but am determined to get him ready. My dick is nowhere near porn-star size. I'm probably pretty average, but I know even three of my thick fingers won't prepare him for the burn.

Apparently, he doesn't care.

"Fuck. Enough. Alec, please."

There's no jesting, no teasing. I can't. Need

guides me with a shaky hand to sheathe myself, pour on lube, and press against his entrance.

"Fuck, yes." Patrick wraps his legs around me. And while he's still trembling, when I nudge and breach him for the first time, a wave of emotion crosses his features before settling into something that takes my breath away.

The calm peering back at me is unexpected. It speaks of rightness and blissed-out perfection, wrapped in acceptance.

I sink deeper. Patrick's eyes widen before they roll back, head pressing into the pillow. A loud, guttural groan tears out of him, and I don't stop, continuing to ease in until I'm balls deep and know I've finally found my place in the world.

With his mouth parted on a silent gasp, Patrick arches his neck, the column strained. A pulse of desire hits me square in the chest. I have to move, tear the sounds clear from him. Drink in his cries. Watch him unravel for me.

With every inch of control I possess, I slide back, easing out of him so slowly, I feel every millimetre of movement in the snugness surrounding me. The drag out has Patrick's gaze snapping to my face. Desperation is in the depths of his whiskey-brown eyes. I know it, feel it completely.

"I need—"

I cut off his words when I slam back in. His groan is immediate.

"Yes!"

Dragging out steadily again causes him to clamp down on me, as if worried I'll pull out for good, and I ram back in. His cry tells me this is what he wants. What he needs.

There's nothing tentative about my movements. No gentle sway and grind. I can't, not when he's scrambling for purchase on my waist, urging me on, calling out "Harder." I plunge deep, pleasure a sweet siren call, begging me to take what I want and give him everything he needs.

Picking up the pace, I pound into him, adjusting the cant of my hips. I have to find that place inside him that will unravel him completely. Need it more than my next breath. Need it so desperately, to hear Patrick scream in pleasure before I fall apart and spill.

"So fucking hot." The words are grunted between my gritted teeth.

"Keep going." He's nodding almost frantically, movements untamed as he meets each drive into him.

Heat tingles my skin as I power forwards, reaching for his cock just as he gasps, "Fuck, there, there."

"Fuck." Finally. Satisfaction blurs my vision as I keep up with the angle. He groans and moans and cusses up a storm. I memorise every sound. Memorise the flush of his cheeks, the way his head rocks side to side, the stretch of the column of his neck.

Gripping his cock, I slide my still-slick fingers over his heated skin. A fresh grunt tears free from his open mouth.

"Jesus. You're so fucking amazing." My words are breathless as I drink him in, trying like hell to tip him over the edge.

His fingers dig into my hips, bruising and perfect. I welcome the bite, the pinch, the absolute reminder of it being Patrick who's taking me so perfectly, without restraint or inhibition, and making me absolutely his.

"Fuck, fuck, fuck." The words are a chant, the precursor to Patrick's body locking tight as I grind deep into his arse and still, pushing against his prostate until he's spilling in my hand.

I don't pause. Don't stop working his cock, milking him dry, and with two more pumps of my hips, I finally fall. Drop into an abyss of heat and light and perfection. A long groan rips out of my chest as my body stutters and I fill the latex.

I revel in the feeling of ecstasy, rejoice in Patrick

coming undone, and bask in the glow of orgasming so hard, the stars blurring my vision rival those of any Queensland sky.

Spent and skin tingling, I ease down, barely holding myself up on my forearms. With my face buried against his neck, I breathe heavily, dragging in air and the scent of Patrick and sex. "That was…" My muscles ripple, coming down from the high of my orgasm. Unable to land on the right word to finish my thought, I instead press light kisses along his neck, up his throat, and make my way to his lips.

He kisses me back, closed-mouthed and simply sinking into the contact. Our chests are still heaving, and I know I need to move to let him breathe properly, but pulling away is a challenge. When he shifts a little beneath me, I know it's time, so I reluctantly ease back and prop up my jelly-like arms.

"Hey." A goofy-arse grin morphs on my face, and he smiles back when he takes it in.

"Hey." He angles up and gives me a whisper of a kiss. "You okay?"

"Amazing." I search his gaze, trying to read the emotions that he displays so freely. "You were perfect, and fuck… that was everything."

His gaze softens as he listens. "*You* were perfect."

I swear I'm close to seeing love hearts appear

above my head, and I'm sure I'm peering down at him with a sappy expression. I'm so okay with that.

He shifts again, reminding me of where my cock's buried and of the cooling spunk wedged between us.

"You want to grab a shower?"

"Definitely."

I ease out of him, hold onto the ends of the condom, and watch his face carefully. There's a wince, but when he sees my attention, he smiles, saying, "I'm fine. It's just been a while. Totally worth it."

Confident he wouldn't bullshit me, I nod and help him out of bed. I chuckle at my shaking legs. "My legs feel like jelly."

"Good. It means we did something right." He's smiling as he leads me out of his room towards the bathroom.

When I stop him short, he angles back, eyebrows raised in question. "All okay?"

"Yeah." I clear my throat, my gaze shifting to the rumpled sheets and the uncapped lube. "Just wondering if we needed the lube and another condom."

Surprise floods his features, swiftly followed by amusement. "Not sure my arse can wi—"

"The condom's for you," I say quickly. Hell, just

the thought of him inside me has my dick taking interest.

"Yeah?" The question sounds strangled.

"Fuck yes. You buried inside me, shooting your load—" My body trembles and I swallow hard. "The only thing better will be when we can go bare so I can feel you filling me up." I'm practically panting by the time I've finished speaking. I want that so fucking badly.

"Fucking hell." He tugs me close, his mouth finding purchase as he devours me. It's frantic and messy, fucking sinful, and I love that I've made him lose control.

By the time he releases me, my knees wobble, and he races to his drawer, picking up supplies, before hauling me to the bathroom where I know he'll make good on every fantasy I've ever had.

CHAPTER 14

PATRICK

IT'S BEEN THREE DAYS SINCE EASTER SATURDAY. Three days since Alec claimed me as his—and I claimed him right back. Three days since he declared we were in a relationship.

"You're doing it again."

Not bothering to act ignorant, or even innocent, I simply shrug, my loved-up smile stretching even wider. "Don't care." I lean into Alec, press my face against his neck, and inhale.

We've been on the go all day, so he should stink, but all I smell are the faint traces of my shower gel, my body spray that he's taken to using, and the fresh sweat of a hard-working man.

He huffs a laugh and squirms as I step behind

him, carrying on inhaling and dotting kisses along the sweet taste of his neck. When he relaxes against me, I rest my chin on his shoulder and peer out into the distance.

We're standing at one of the fence lines a few paddocks away from the house, Trev having left us alone while he washes up. Having just finished replacing a few termite-infested posts and reslotting the barbed wire, we're tired and grubby. But standing here like this, soaking in the sun that's still about an hour from setting, I've never seen a sky look so perfect over my family's property.

"It really is beautiful here."

"I know." A pang of longing for what could be squeezes my chest. I don't believe for one second Alec's exaggerating how he feels about this place, but it's a long way from his life back on the coast and the type of life he leads. Plus there's the whole fact I work wherever the mining company sends me, and on a two-on-two-off roster. The shift isn't known to be kind to married couples, let alone new relationships.

The air is still. With the April heat finally feeling more seasonal, it's perfect out. Sure, it's still a warm twenty-eight degrees Celsius in the day, but the evenings are drawing in, dropping quickly to fourteen or so at night. Before we know it, winter will swing around, and the days will be deliciously warm, the nights sometimes dropping to below zero, just to make sure we light our wood burners.

I have no idea if I'll be here in winter—my dad's progress and what's going to happen are still up in the air—but eighteen years of growing up here taught me enough that a Roma winter is my favourite time of year.

"What are you thinking about?" Alec turns his head, indicating for me to shift back. I do so reluctantly but am happy when he faces me and hooks his fingers in my belt loops.

"That winter will be here before you know it." When his lips twitch, I roll my eyes. "Yes, yes, I'm a regular Jon Snow."

A loud, abrupt laugh spills from him, filling the space between us.

Damn, I love his laugh. The sound. The way it morphs his features into a thing of beauty.

"You like winter here?"

I bob my head and tell him what I was just thinking.

"I can see you liking that time of year. It's one of my favourites too."

"Footie season?"

"Ha. Maybe it has a little to do with it. It tends to be busy at work, though, with the extra-curricular stuff, plus there's the league training."

It's an unpleasant reminder that he leaves this week and will be going back to work on Monday. His evenings will be busy preparing lessons, though I imagine it's a relief he teaches PE and not English or something. But what time he wins with the lack of marking and more is spent during breaks and after school.

"That's straight away, right, when you get back?"

"Yeah." Some of his enthusiasm disappears. "Pretty much every weekend for the next few months the kids I coach have a match, and I run their training sessions too. I think till about September."

Shifting his hands to my waist, he squeezes when I remain quiet. Understanding shines in his eyes.

"You know, the whole 'relationship' thing you keep grinning about," he says with a lopsided smirk, "I wasn't bullshitting."

Loud, fast thuds strike my chest. It looks like we're finally doing this, talking about the reality of what happens next. Something I've been actively avoiding, and I think he has too. "I know." I loop my arms around him so I can press my mouth against his.

I'm seeking comfort and reassurance, but there's no avoiding this conversation.

After a gentle kiss, I ease away. "I want that too." For so damn long. I don't remind him of how long he's been it for me. He's got a good idea, since I've spent years flirting with him.

"We'll get it figured out. Video calls will help, plus, your work schedule will make things easier."

A tendril of relief unfurls in my stomach. That he views my work schedule as something positive is a good thing. "You're right." I aim for confident and upbeat, but by his tender smile, I'm not sure he's buying it.

"How long have you wanted this?" He's teasing, so I force my shoulders to relax and quirk my brow.

"*This* being?"

A light pinch precedes him saying, "Me, arsehole. How long?"

"Since the moment you winked at me and flipped Trevor off before dive bombing in your parents' pool."

His lips part and he doesn't hide his surprise.

"Those tiny blue Speedos you were wearing may have something to do with it."

He closes his mouth, pink filling his cheeks. "You remember that? Those?"

I chuckle. "You in Speedos was spank bank material for years." I'm not even joking.

He's flustered as he shakes his head, staring at me a little wide-eyed. "In my defence," he says, and I see him pull himself together, the teasing smile I know and love appearing on lips that get me revved up, especially when he's sucking my dick, "that day I'd spent the morning swim training, hence the budgie smugglers."

"You remember that day?"

When he bobs his head, blood rushes to my brain, making me a little light-headed. "Yeah. You got to Mum and Dad's while I was out training. But we should be talking about what *you* were wearing." There's amused accusation in his tone.

"Me?"

"Yes, you. With your hot Billabong boardies. They were so tight on your arse, I didn't know which way to look."

A jolt of adrenalin strikes me. "You noticed my arse?" There's no mistaking my confusion.

"How could I not? It was right there."

Bemused, I shake my head, sporting a half smile. "You know, most straight guys don't notice or struggle to look away from men's arses."

His gaze searches mine, a flicker of heat

appearing in the depths of his brown eyes. "I think it's safe to say I'm not straight." His smile is sweet, hovering between amused and shy. "I've always been…" There's a pause. "…aware of you, and in Bali that changed to something…" He seems to struggle for the right word.

"Unexpected?" I offer.

"Amazing." His tone is soft, reverent, and hell if longing doesn't swell to the size of a tsunami. I'll happily let it sweep me away if it'll lead me to sharing a life with Alec.

Leaning forwards, I press my forehead to his, soaking in the moment. "We're going to be okay." Steel, wishes, hope—all three are threaded into the words.

"There's no doubt in my mind." He punctuates his assurance with a kiss and turns around so he's back in my arms and we continue to watch the lowering sun.

A flourish of colour begins to spread as each minute passes, painting the darkening blue with burnt oranges and wisps of yellow. The sunset is beautiful, but it's the stars we're interested in.

Even on cloudy nights and when storms threaten, they're still there. Just out of reach and hidden from view. But they're not going anywhere. They'll still sparkle, shine, and blaze, drawing our focus to them so we can continue to turn our gazes up and get lost in their beauty and the vastness of their home.

It's under the blazing stars we found each other. And as long as they keep lighting up the night sky, Alec and I will be just fine.

EPILOGUE

ALEC

The sound of banging boots is the alarm clock I never knew I wanted. At least this wake-up call comes with the kettle being boiled and bread being put in the toaster. With a stretch, I smile. Bones crack, joints pop, and my loud yawn gets Basil's attention.

Our border collie is broken. I'm convinced of it.

Rather than joining Patrick doing his rounds on the property this morning, Basil is much more interested in sleeping in and overheating my feet. At least Petal's not here, stinking up our bedroom with her toxic farts.

When Patrick dragged himself out of bed at the arse crack of dawn this morning, I was sure Petal, our cattle dog, was going to hyperventilate with excitement. She must have known Patrick was checking on the cows.

It's calving season, and there are a handful of cows Patrick's concerned about. Hence the early wake up.

"We best get up before Patrick drags us out of bed."

While Basil's ears perk up, he doesn't move his head. He won't until I'm fully committed and both my feet are on the floor.

"Okay, I'm getting up."

The ear twitch suggests Basil doesn't believe me. Understandable, really. It's the second day of the summer holiday. Seven blissful weeks of no school and nothing but working on the property, having the occasional lie-in, and getting as much downtime as possible. Including a cheeky long-overdue trip overseas.

And all with my handsome husband.

Hearing a door close, I clamber out of bed. At my movement, Basil leaps off the mattress and races to the closed door, tail wagging.

"Hold on." A few steps later, I let him out, then head to our en suite to take a piss, wash up, and brush my teeth.

By the time I reach the kitchen, my coffee's made.

A second later, I'm wrapped around Patrick. "Morning." I dot a kiss on the back of his neck. Since he doesn't stink of farm, I assume everything was okay this morning. "Girls okay?"

As always, Patrick snorts. "Cattle," he says, turning so he can capture my mouth and give me a proper good-morning kiss. I'm breathless by the time he pulls away and almost prepared to agree with everything he says. Only almost, though. Maybe if he dropped to his knees that would be a definitely.

"You're thinking something dirty." He bounces his brows, seemingly super impressed with himself.

"Will that be *this*"—I shove my boner against his groin—"giving me away?"

He groans at the contact, and I give myself a mental pat on the back for drawing the sound from him. His moans and groans, especially when they're super needy, are some of my favourite sounds. They were five years ago, almost to the day of when we finally hooked up in Bali, just like they were a little over four years ago when I listened to my gut, quit my job, and moved out to Roma.

Because of course this is where we landed.

Rather than going back to work after his dad's injury, Patrick made the decision to stay put, care for Graham during his long recovery, and run the property. In truth, it made those eight months we were apart while navigating our relationship unbelievably hard. There were no two-week breaks where I could steal him away and keep him tied to my bed.

By July, I'd handed in my notice. By November I was wondering what the hell I'd done, as a position still hadn't become available in one of the two schools in Roma, but thank Christ by January, two weeks before the start of a new school year, and when I'd already moved, James reached out to me saying a position had become vacant.

I'd nearly wept in relief, and for the first time appreciated how shitty the education system was that someone could change their mind about a teaching job just two weeks before the start of school.

"Uh-huh. Just maybe," Patrick says as he grabs my arse cheeks, giving a tight squeeze.

"Bloody hell. Keep the groping to a minimum before I've had my coffee, boys." Graham pushes open the flyscreen door, rolls his eyes at us, then cuddles our two dogs that he absolutely, definitely didn't want us to have. "How's the calving coming along?" he asks, giving Petal a kiss on her snout.

Patrick doesn't release me. I half-heartedly squirm to move, but when he looks at me pointedly, I stop, realising I still feel our hard dicks pushed up against each other.

"All good. Two heifers. Looks like they just arrived. Both are already up and feeding."

"Did you take photos?" Seriously, new-born calves are the cutest. I wait patiently for Patrick to answer, but narrow my gaze when he—

"Yes." He rolls his eyes, pretending he doesn't find my love for calves adorable. Tugging out his phone, he hands it over. When he does, he releases me and turns back to the toaster, just in time to hear the pop.

"Thank you." I nuzzle his back, type in his pin code, and ooh and ahh over the photographs. "They're super cute. You want to see, Graham?"

With a chuckle, Graham makes his way to the large kitchen table. Half of it's covered in crap—not literally crap, obviously, just all the shit we dump there when we can't be arsed to put it away. "I'm good, thanks, Alec. When you've seen thousands, you've seen them all."

I glance up in time to see his soft, amused smile aimed at me.

Admittedly, I don't make the best cattle farmer. The whole sending them to the market, or the meat works, or even calling in the butcher to put a cow in a freezer are times I legit find a reason to go to school or meet up with one of my mates. That doesn't mean I don't help however I can. But if there's a choice between hand-rearing a calf whose mum abandons them or hearing a shotgun when the butcher's around, it's a no-brainer that I go for the cute calves every damn time.

"You about ready for your trip?" Graham asks.

"Yeah. I think so. We're all packed at least." I turn to Patrick. "You sorted?"

He bobs his head, picks up a plate of buttered toast, and places it on the table. "Pretty much. I just need to call Yarran about a couple of things, then we're good to head to the airport." He takes a seat as I set the side plates down and pass Graham his doctored coffee.

"Bloody ridiculous to think I need someone to come and check up on me." Graham's been sulking about this since we told him about our seven-night trip to Bali and that Yarran was going to stay while we were away.

"Dad, we've been over this." Patrick picks up his coffee. "It's not about Yarran checking up on you. You're obviously more than capable, but with Ness now working full-time and John working too, it's a good idea to have an extra pair of hands, especially with calving."

It took a long time, pretty much a year, for Graham to be active again after his surgery. What didn't help was his arthritis flare-up. And while he's young in the grand scheme of things, he's still in his sixties, and this property takes a lot of work. Something he conveniently forgets when he chooses.

"I know."

Patrick and I glance at each other, not sure where this acceptance has come from rather than his usual petulant response.

"So you won't be an arsehole to him, then?" Patrick asks, and I bite my lip to stop myself from laughing.

The unimpressed look Graham shoots his way is answer enough, so, sensibly, Patrick changes the subject and talks to his dad about the upcoming cattle market at the sales yards.

I ease back in my chair, munching my toast, sipping my coffee, and petting Petal, who's hovering in case I drop a crumb. When Patrick laughs and Graham joins in, I sigh in contentment, grateful this is my life.

Heading to Bali is a treat, but I'd be just as happy spending the whole summer break here. And as I look at Patrick, whose lips are buttery and smile is bright, I squeeze his palm that settles on my knee. I catch his gaze and take my fill, letting him know with the special look we share that he's my everything.

The sweet smile that he saves just for me tilts his lips. I love this man so much and in every conceivable way. And if there ever was a bucket list, it would be full. How could it not be when Patrick made the promise to always be mine?

***

I hope you found sweet escapism in Alec and Patrick's story. Since creating Alec's character in **HIGH ALERT**—Ross's story—I've been so eager for him to have a story of his own.

Looking for more Aussies romances? Check out **STUMBLE**, a fun, sweet, and sexy romance, taking place on Queensland's Sunshine Coast.

ABOUT THE AUTHOR

I live and breathe all things book related. Usually with at least three books being read and two WiPs being written at the same time, life is merrily hectic. I tend to do nothing by halves, so I happily seek the craziness and busyness life offers.

Living on my small property in Queensland with my human family as well as my animal family of cows, chooks, sheep, and dogs, I really do appreciate the beauty of the world around me and am a believer that love truly is love.

To check for updates head to my website:
https://beccaseymour.com
https://landing.mailerlite.com/webforms/landing/
r9f0i4
Plus, join my Facebook group, which I share with the
awesome Louisa Masters here:
https://www.facebook.com/groups/
rommancewithbeccalouisa/

facebook.com/beccaseymourauthor

twitter.com/beccaseymour_

instagram.com/authorbeccaseymour

tiktok.com/@beccaseymourwrites

bookbub.com/authors/becca-seymour

LOVE ABROAD COLLECTION

STAND-ALONE LOW-ANGST ROMANCES THAT TRAVEL THE GLOBE.

Jax Stuart: Under a Greek Twilight

Robin Knight: Under the Arabian Sky

Morgan Mason: Under the Smoke and Thunder

Rikki Leighton: Under the Twilight Rainfall

Becca Seymour: Under the Blazing Stars

Kelsey Hodge: Under the Northern Lights

T.H. Compton: Under the Alpenglow

Taylor McNiff: Under the Firefly Sky

Rae Marks: Under the Madagascar Moon

9 781922 679840